BENNY AND PENNY

IN

HOW TO SAY GOODBYE

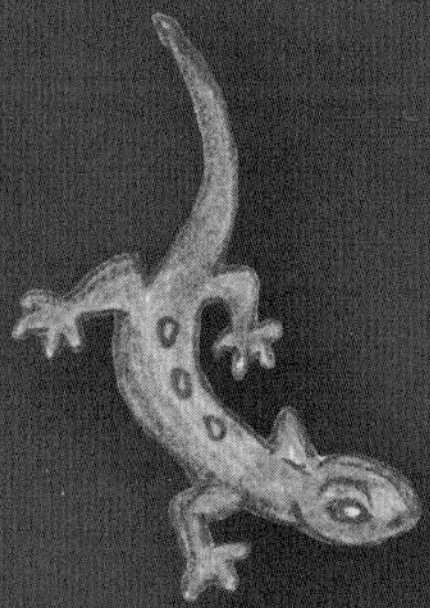

GEOFFREY HAYES

BENNY
AND
PENNY

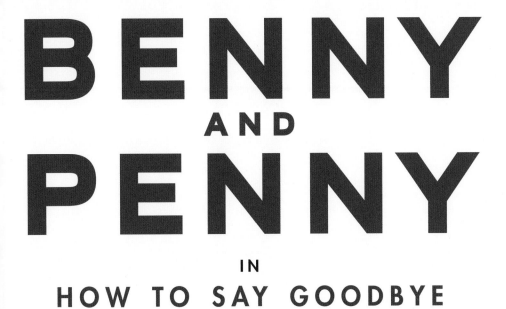

IN

HOW TO SAY GOODBYE

A TOON BOOK BY

GEOFFREY HAYES

For Tomas Grignon — who knows why

Editorial Director & Designer: FRANÇOISE MOULY

GEOFFREY HAYES' artwork was done in colored pencil.

A TOON BOOK

A TOON Book™ © 2016 Geoffrey Hayes & TOON Books, an imprint of Raw Junior, LLC, 27 Greene Street, New York, NY 10013. No part of this book may be used or reproduced in any manner whatsoever without written permission except in the case of brief quotations embodied in critical articles and reviews. TOON Graphics™, TOON Books®, LITTLE LIT® and TOON Into Reading!™ are trademarks of RAW Junior, LLC. All rights reserved. All our books are Smyth Sewn (the highest library-quality binding available) and printed with soy-based inks on acid-free, woodfree paper harvested from responsible sources. Library of Congress Cataloging-in-Publication Data: Names: Hayes, Geoffrey, author, illustrator.   Title: Benny and Penny in How To Say Goodbye : a Toon book / by Geoffrey Hayes   Other titles: How To Say Goodbye   Description: New York, NY : Toon Books, [2016] | Summary: When their salamander friend dies, mouse siblings Benny and Penny learn how to say goodbye.
Identifiers: LCCN 2016003372 | ISBN 9781935179993 (hardback) Subjects: LCSH: Graphic novels. | CYAC: Graphic novels. | Mice--Fiction. | Brothers and sisters--Fiction. | Death--Fiction. | BISAC: JUVENILE FICTION   / Comics & Graphic Novels / General. | JUVENILE FICTION / Social Issues /   Death & Dying. | JUVENILE FICTION / Animals / Mice, Hamsters, Guinea Pigs, etc.| JUVENILE FICTION / Readers / Beginner. Classification: LCC PZ7.7.H39 Bb 2012 | DDC 741.5/973--dc23   LC record available at http://lccn.loc.gov/2016003372
Printed in China by C&C Offset Printing Co., Ltd. Distributed to the trade by Consortium Book Sales; orders (800) 283-3572; orderentry@perseusbooks.com; www.cbsd.com

978-1-935179-99-3 (hardcover)

16 17 18 19 20 21 C&C 10 9 8 7 6 5 4 3 2 1

WWW.TOON-BOOKS.COM

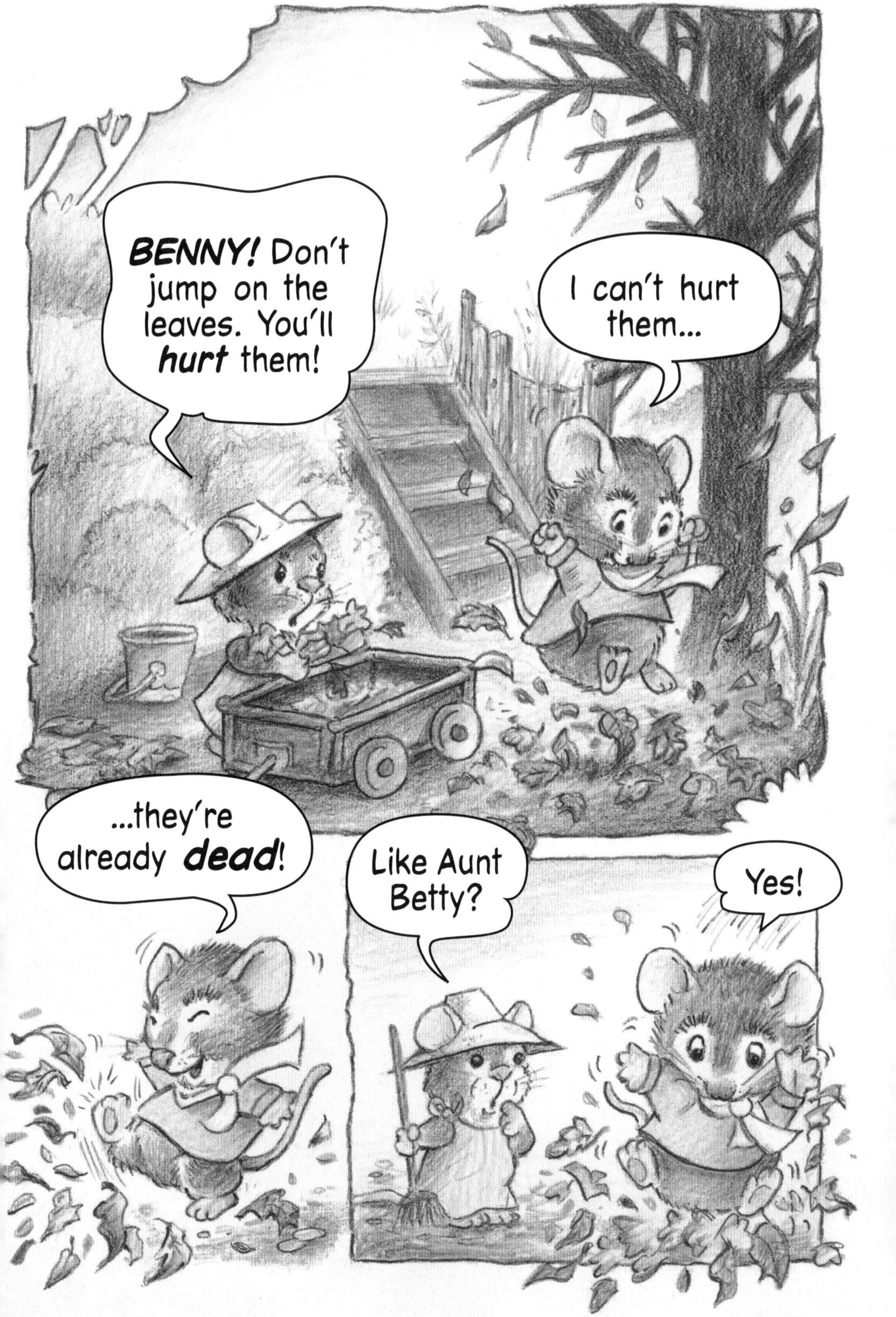
BENNY! Don't jump on the leaves. You'll ***hurt*** them!
I can't hurt them...
...they're already ***dead***!
Like Aunt Betty?
Yes!

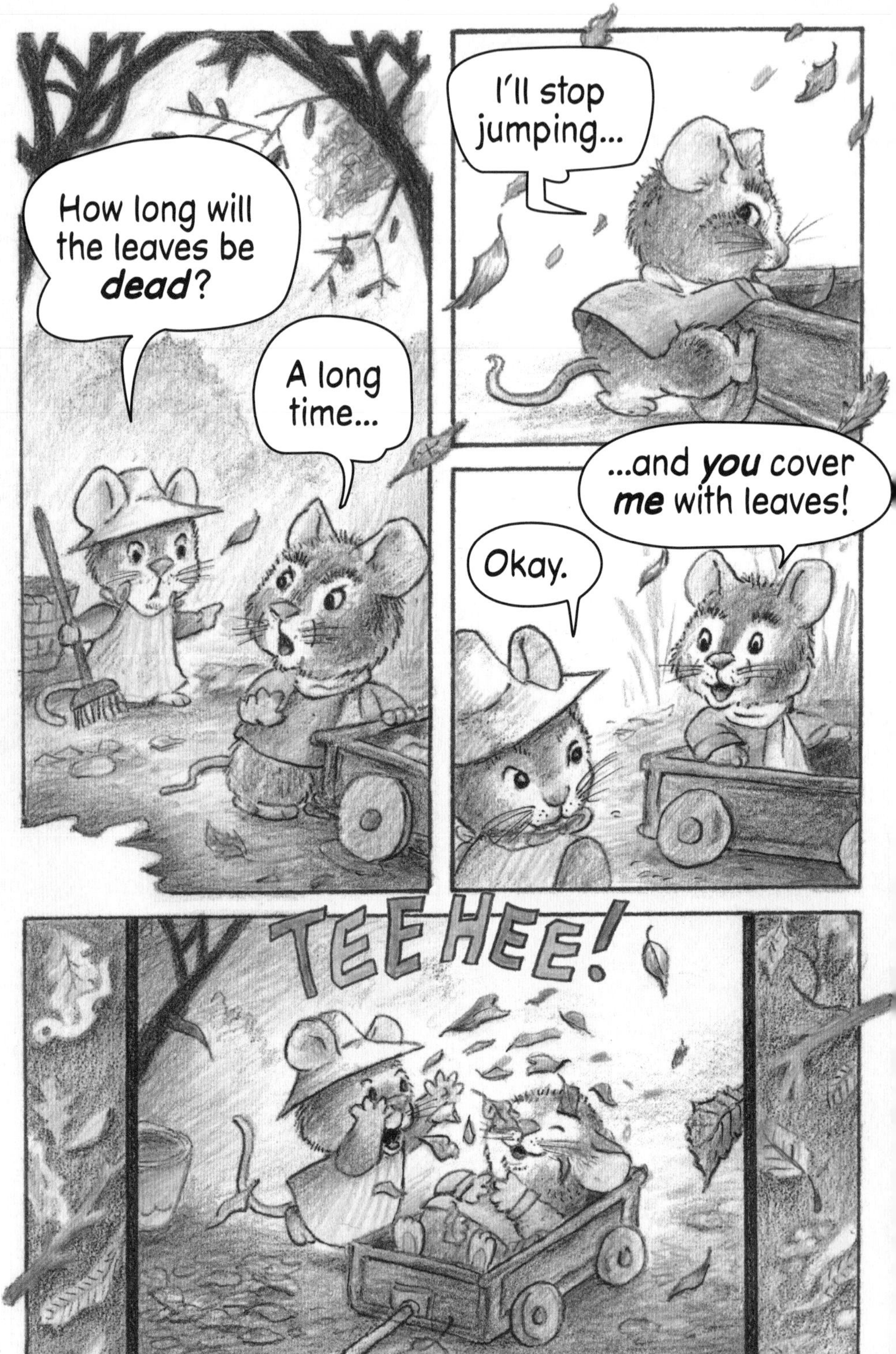
How long will the leaves be *dead*?
A long time...
I'll stop jumping...
Okay.
...and *you* cover *me* with leaves!
TEE HEE!

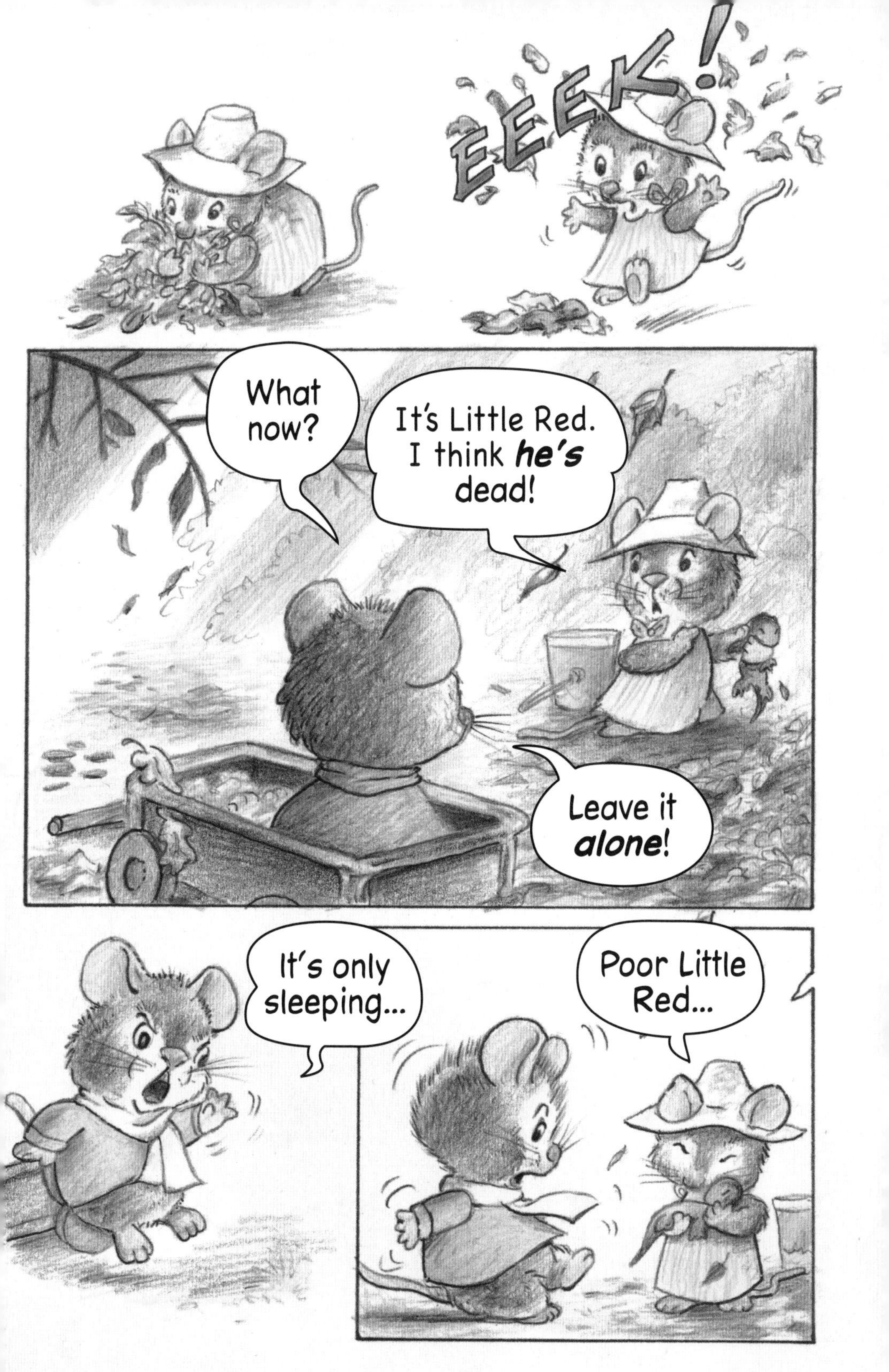
EEEK!
What now?
It's Little Red. I think *he's* dead!
Leave it *alone*!
It's only sleeping...
Poor Little Red...

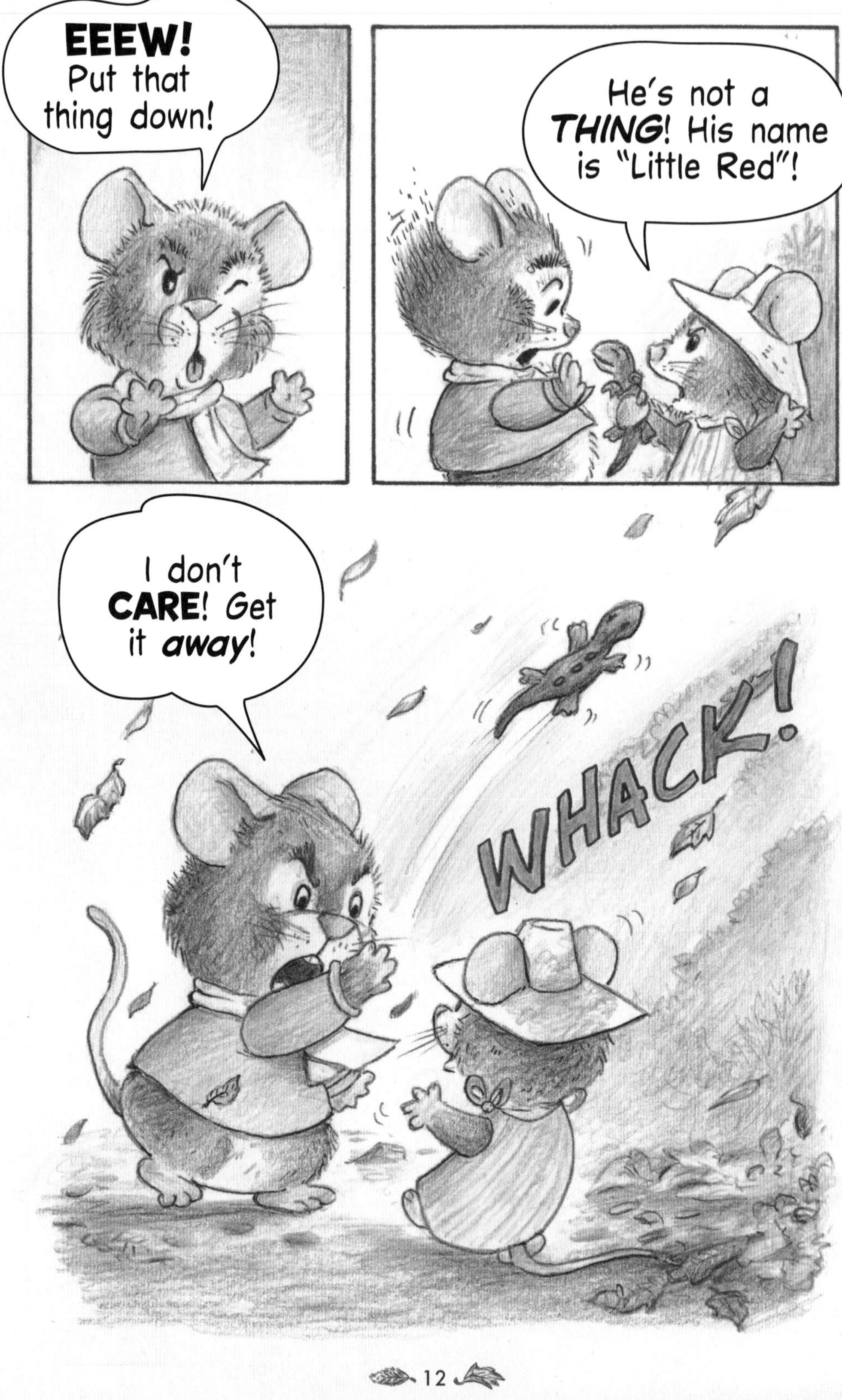
EEEW! Put that thing down!
He's not a THING! His name is "Little Red"!
I don't CARE! Get it away!
WHACK!

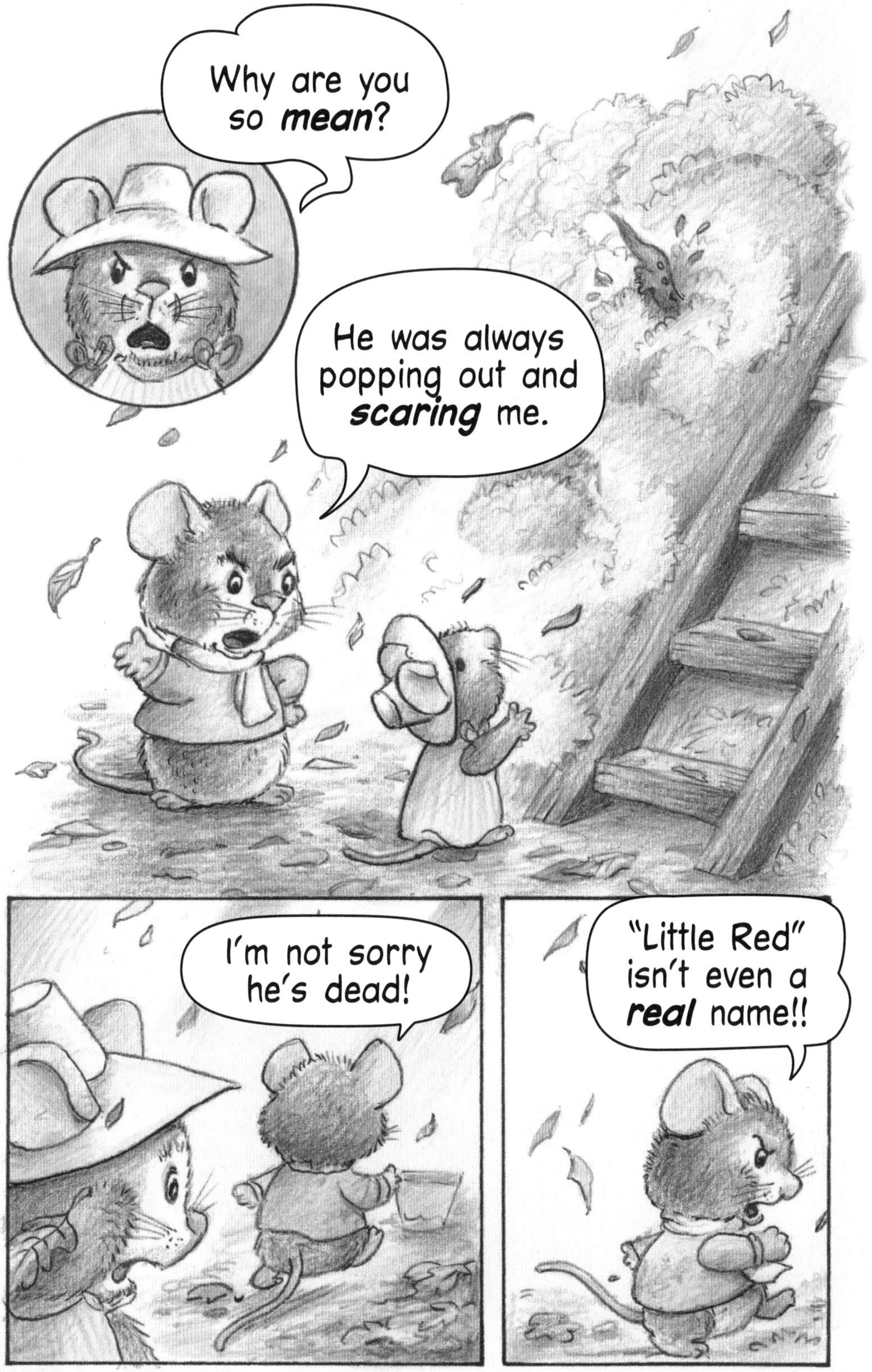
Why are you so *mean*?
He was always popping out and *scaring* me.
I'm not sorry he's dead!
"Little Red" isn't even a *real* name!!

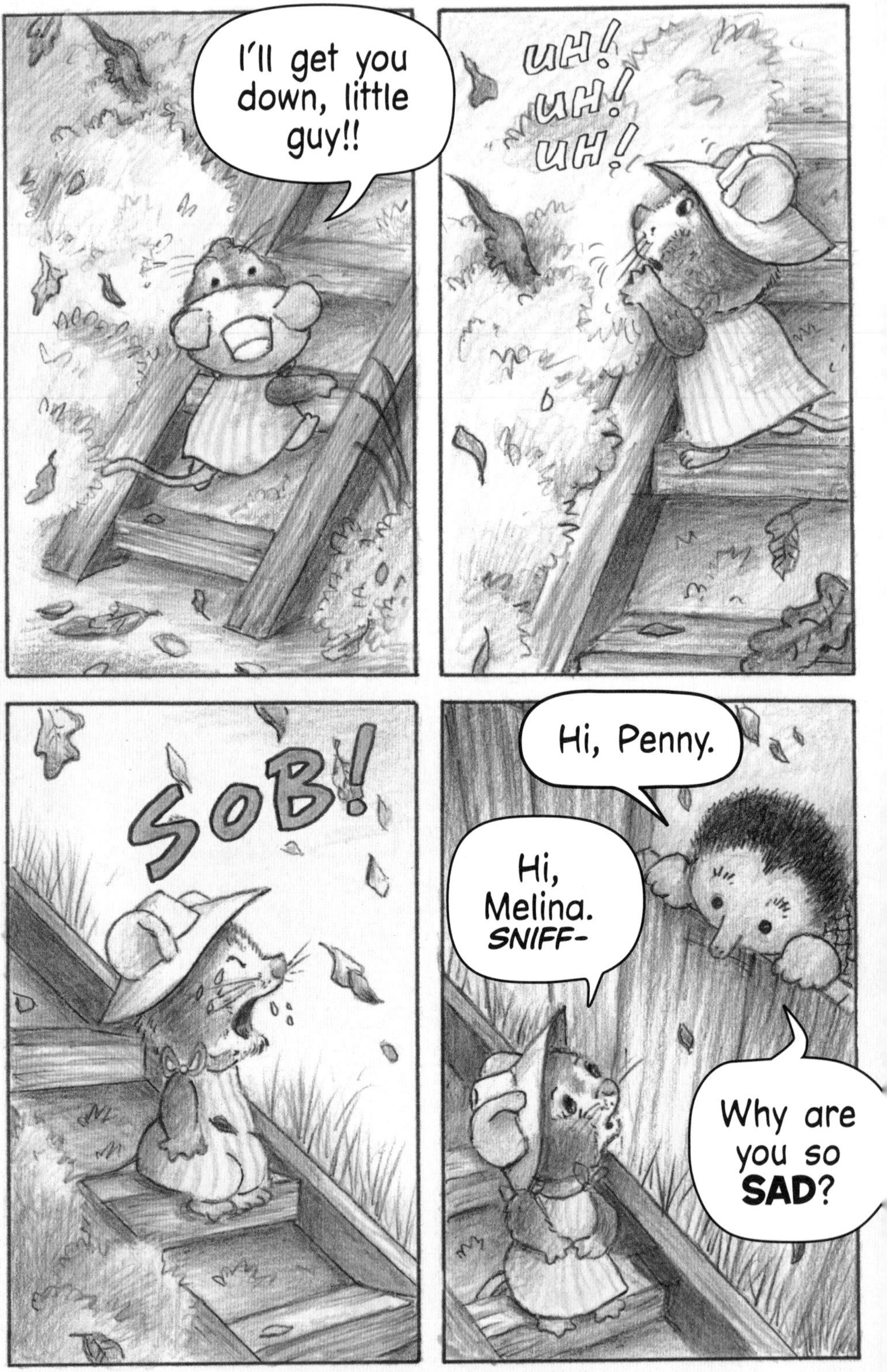
I'll get you down, little guy!!
UH! UH! UH!
SOB!
Hi, Penny.
Hi, Melina. SNIFF-
Why are you so **SAD**?

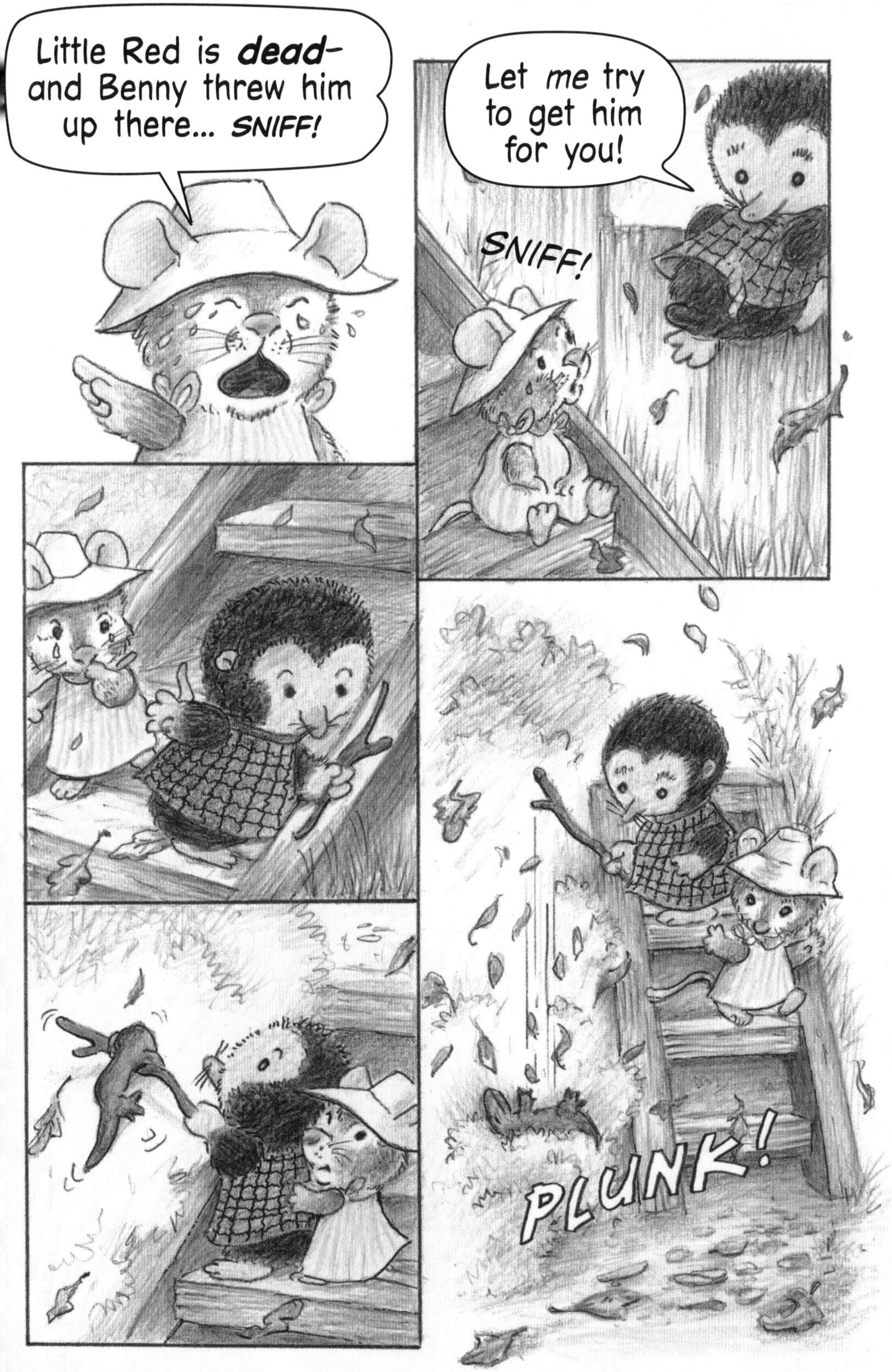
Little Red is *dead*- and Benny threw him up there... SNIFF!
Let *me* try to get him for you!
SNIFF!
PLUNK!

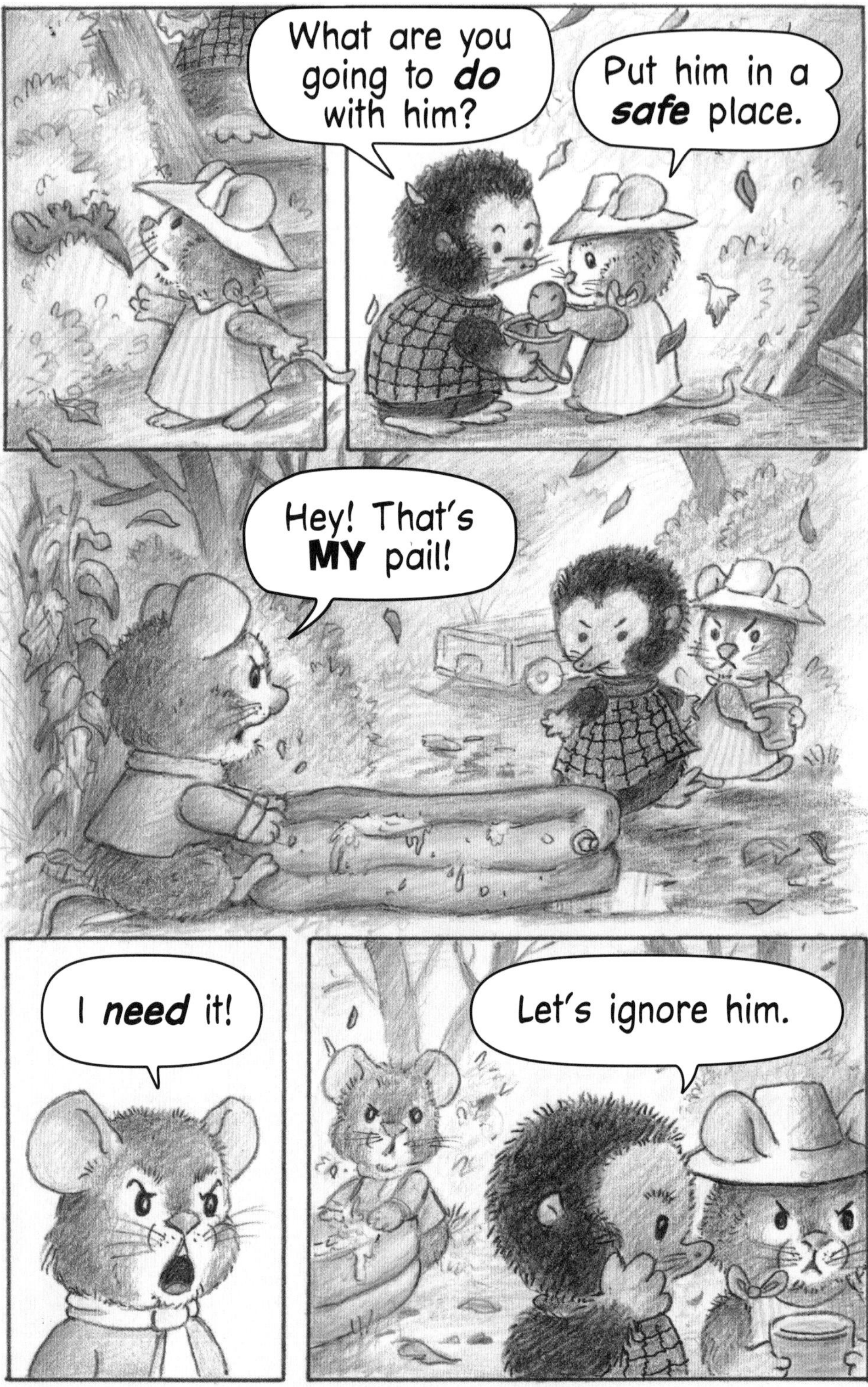
What are you going to ***do*** with him?
Put him in a ***safe*** place.
Hey! That's **MY** pail!
I ***need*** it!
Let's ignore him.

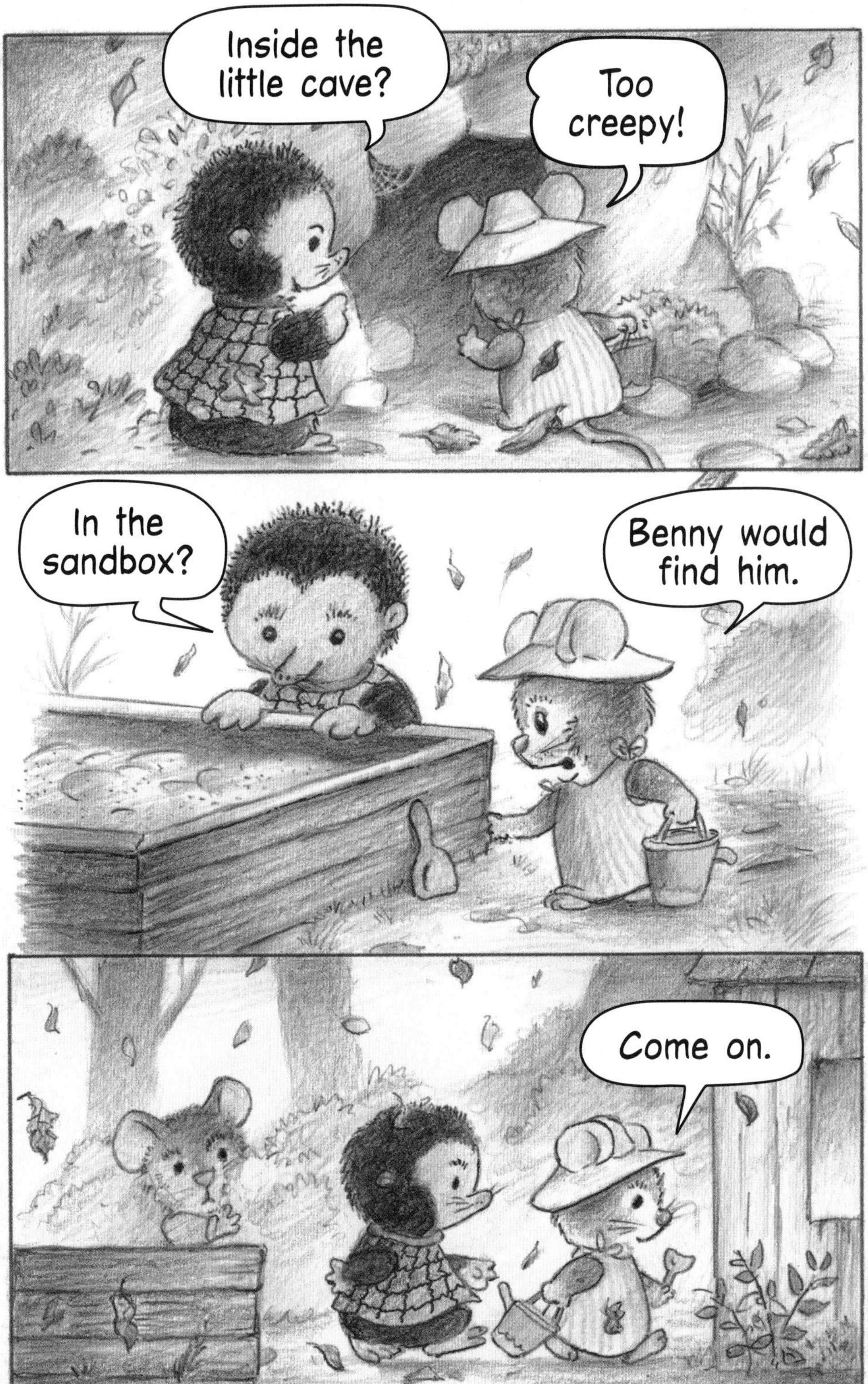
Inside the little cave?
Too creepy!
In the sandbox?
Benny would find him.
Come on.

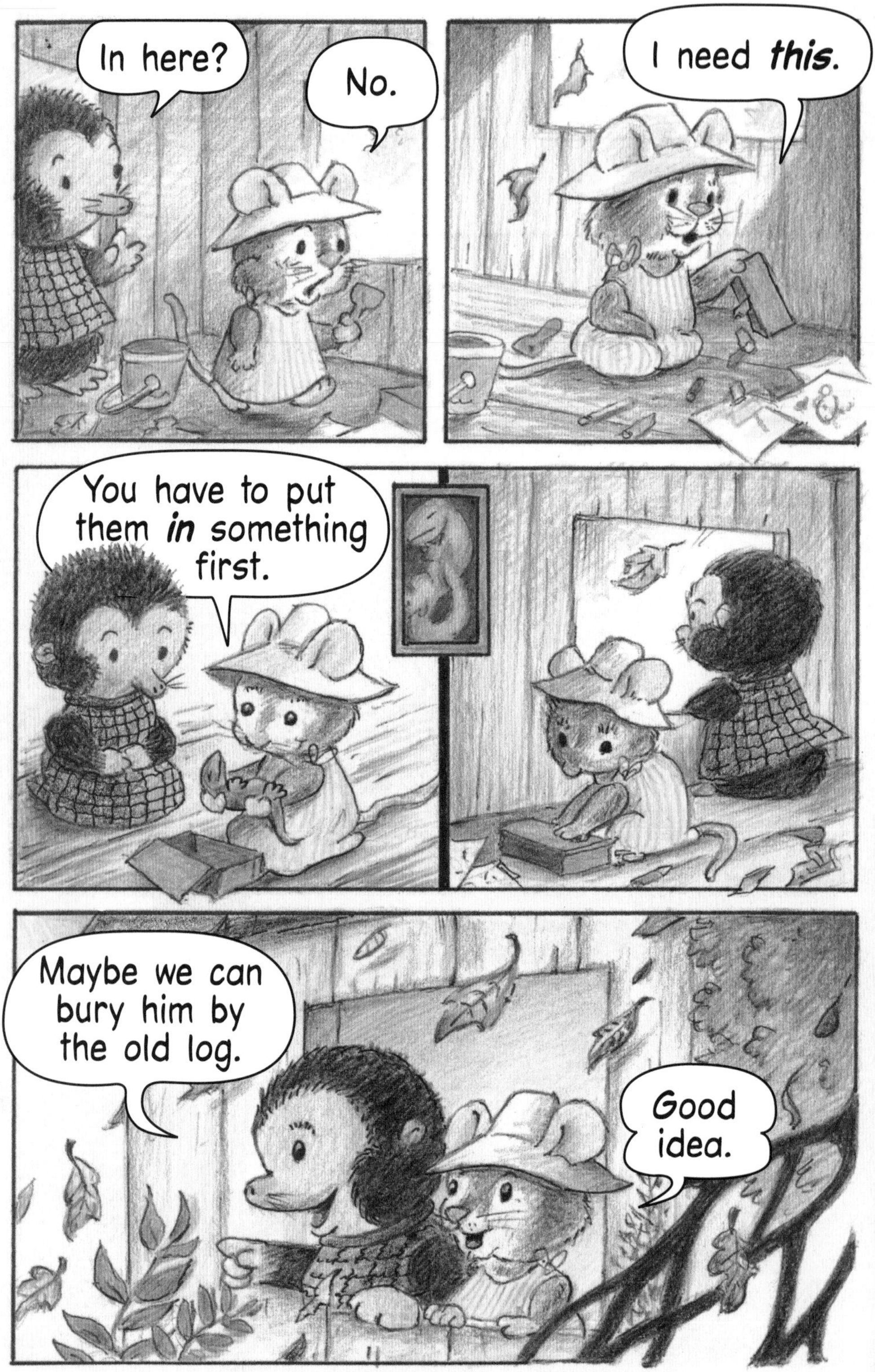
In here?
No.
I need *this*.
You have to put them *in* something first.
Maybe we can bury him by the old log.
Good idea.

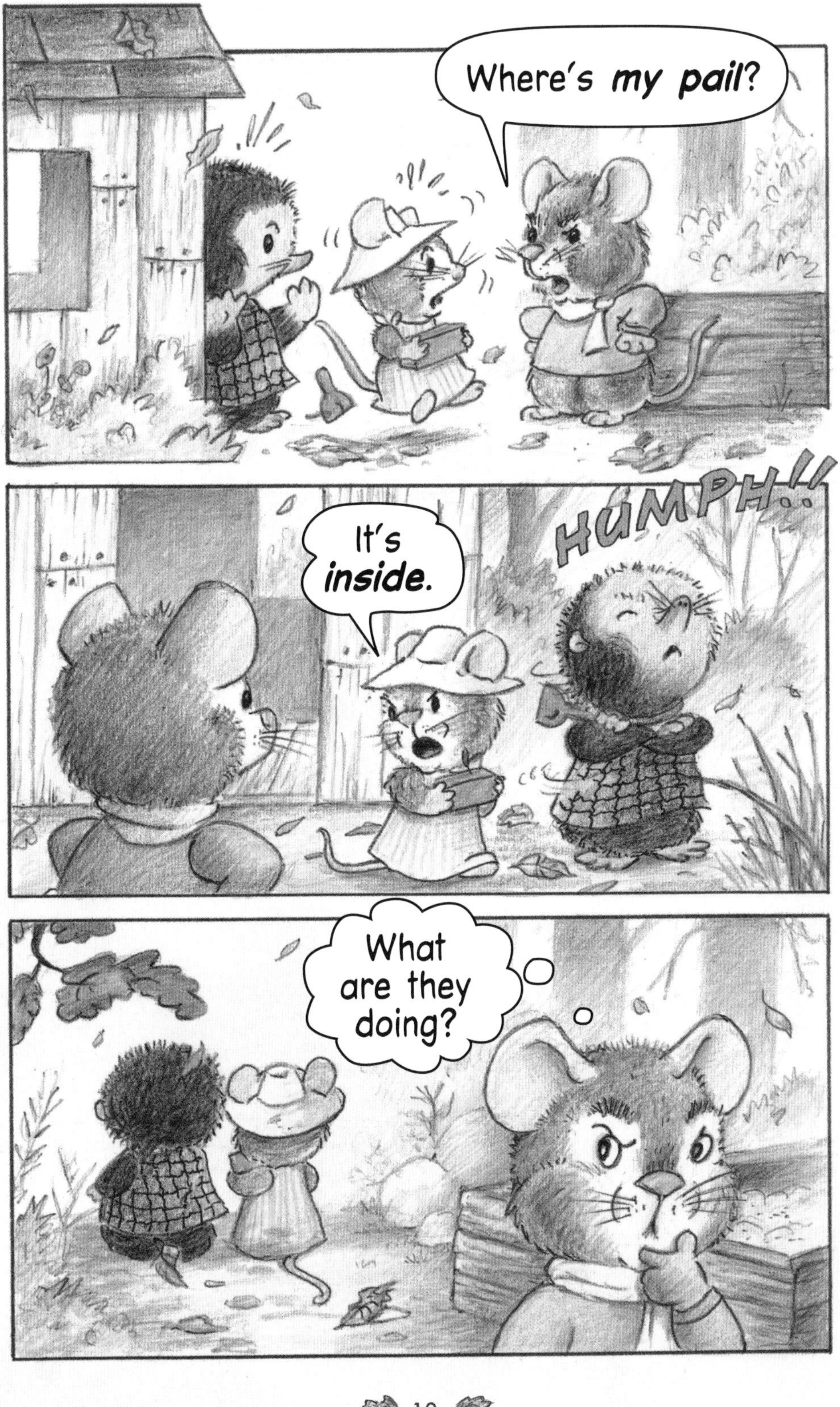
Where's my pail?
It's inside.
HUMPH!!
What are they doing?

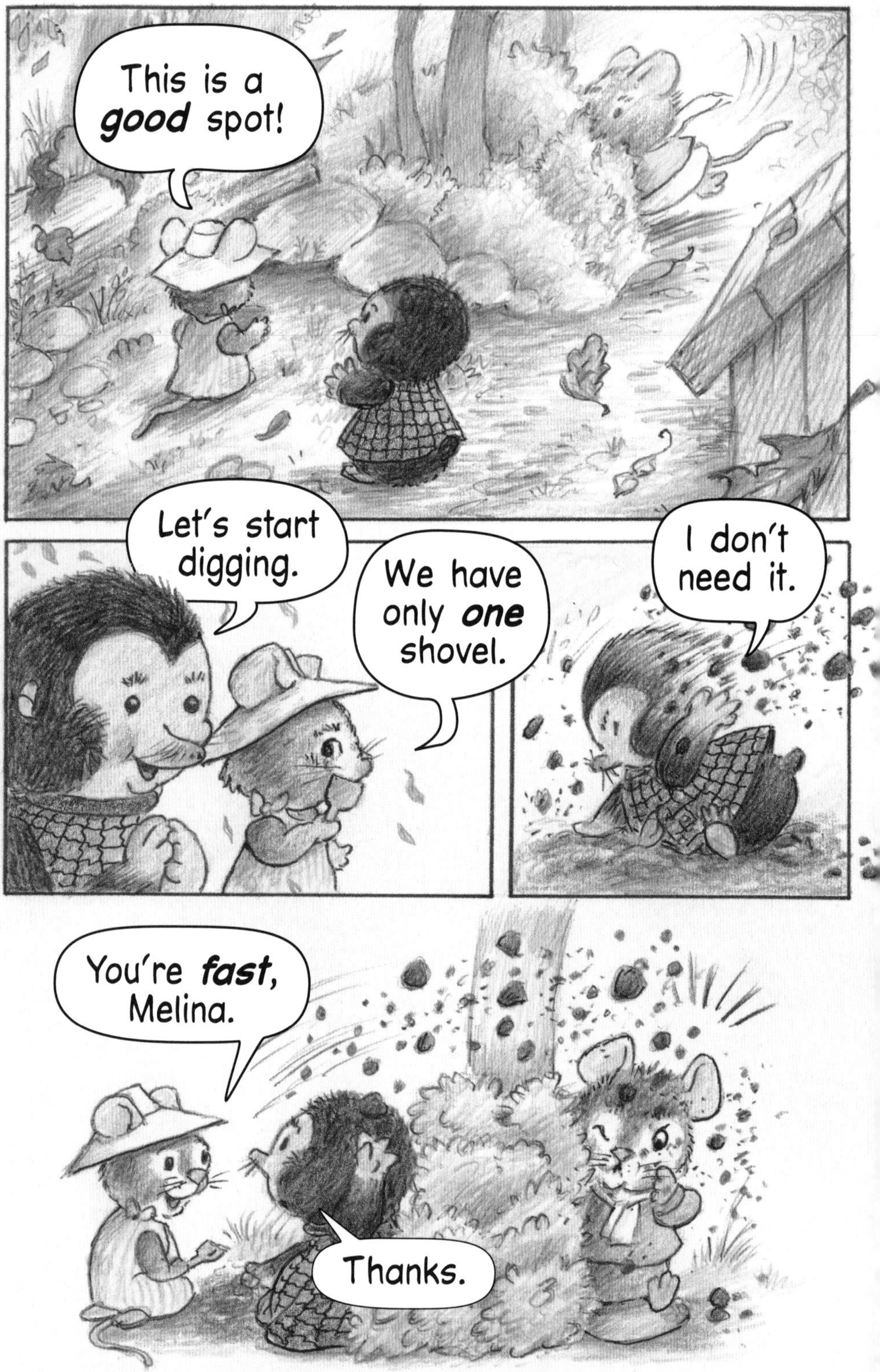
This is a *good* spot!
Let's start digging.
We have only *one* shovel.
I don't need it.
You're *fast*, Melina.
Thanks.

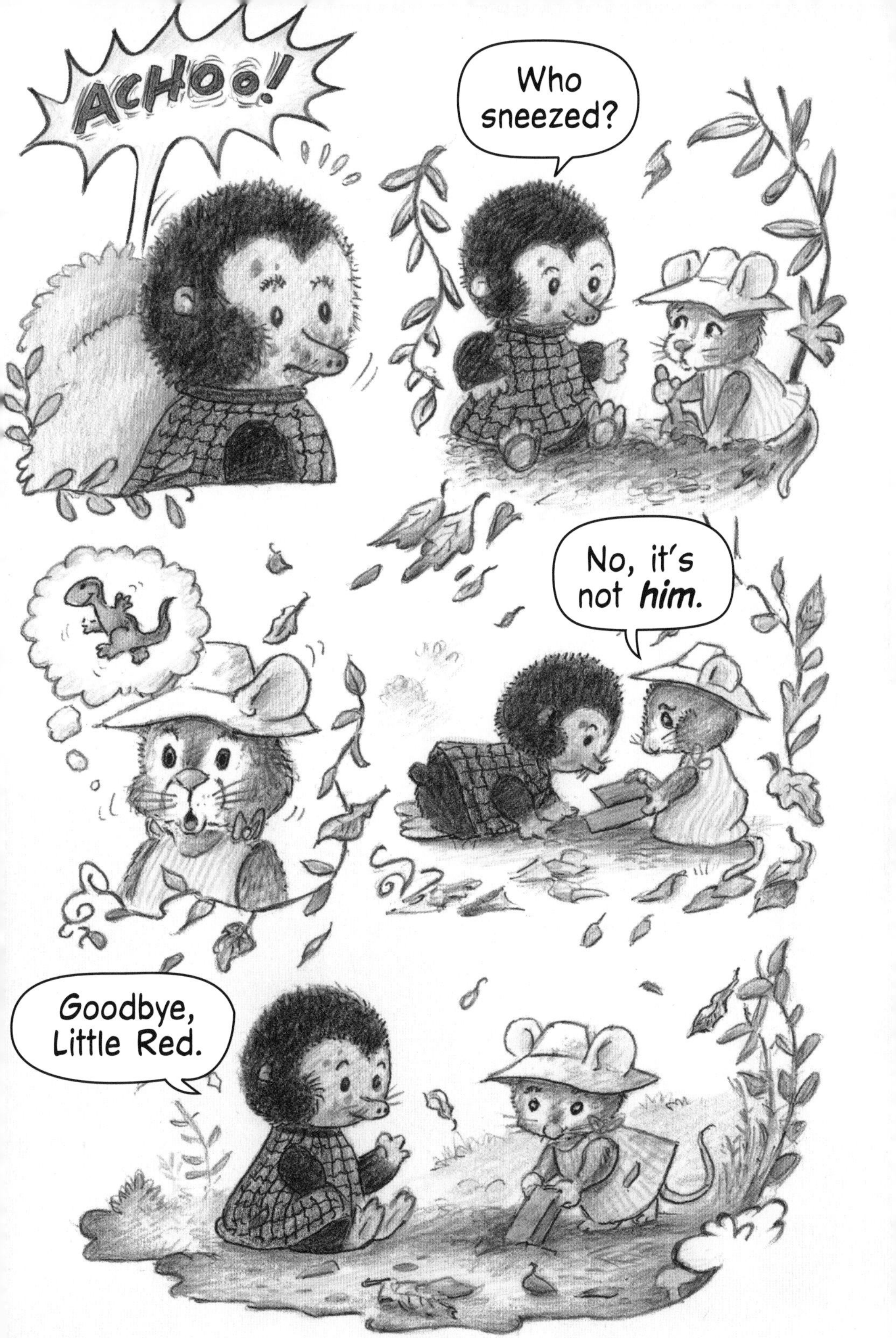
ACHOO!
Who sneezed?
No, it's not ***him***.
Goodbye, Little Red.

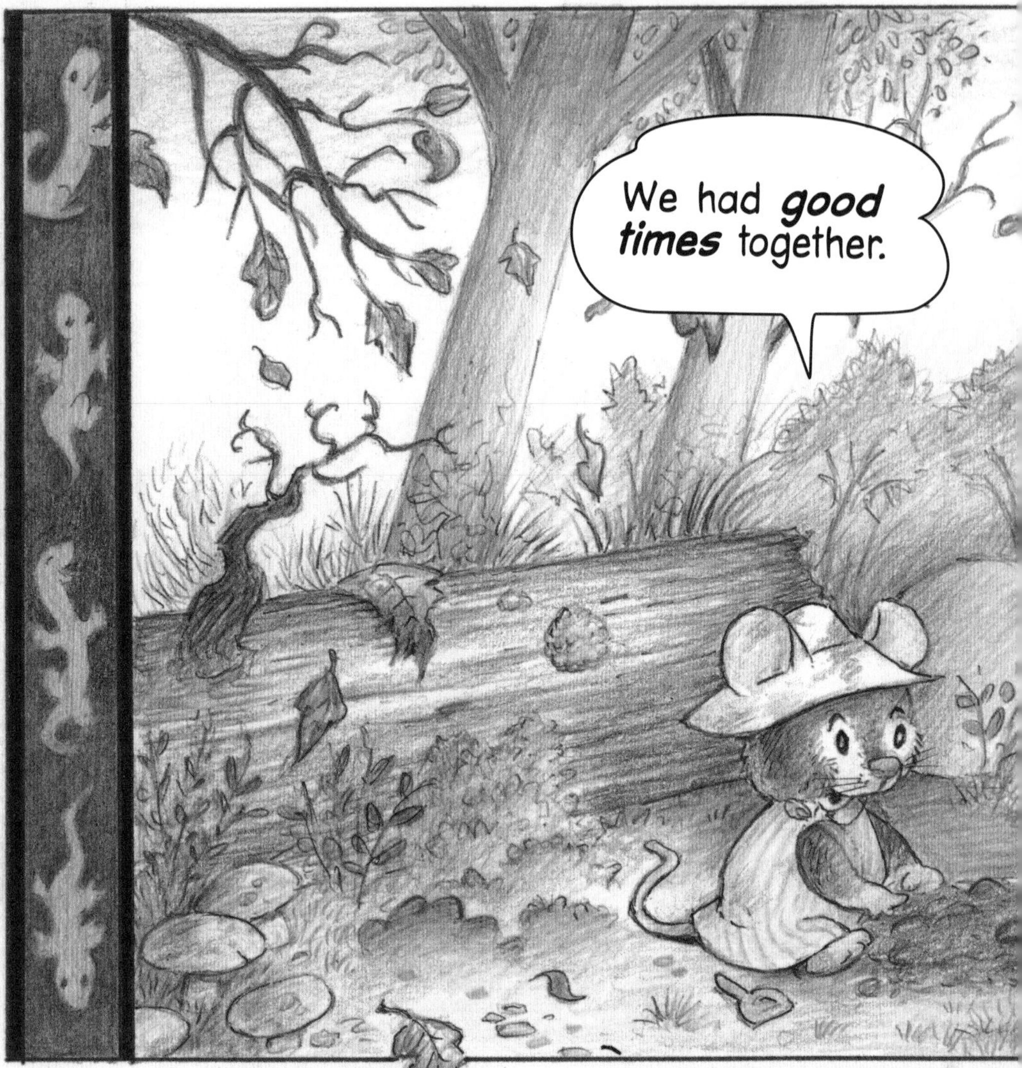
We had ***good times*** together.

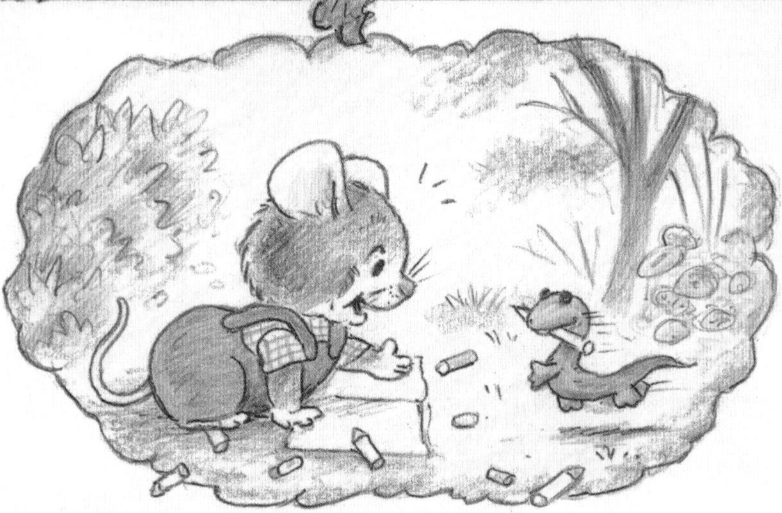

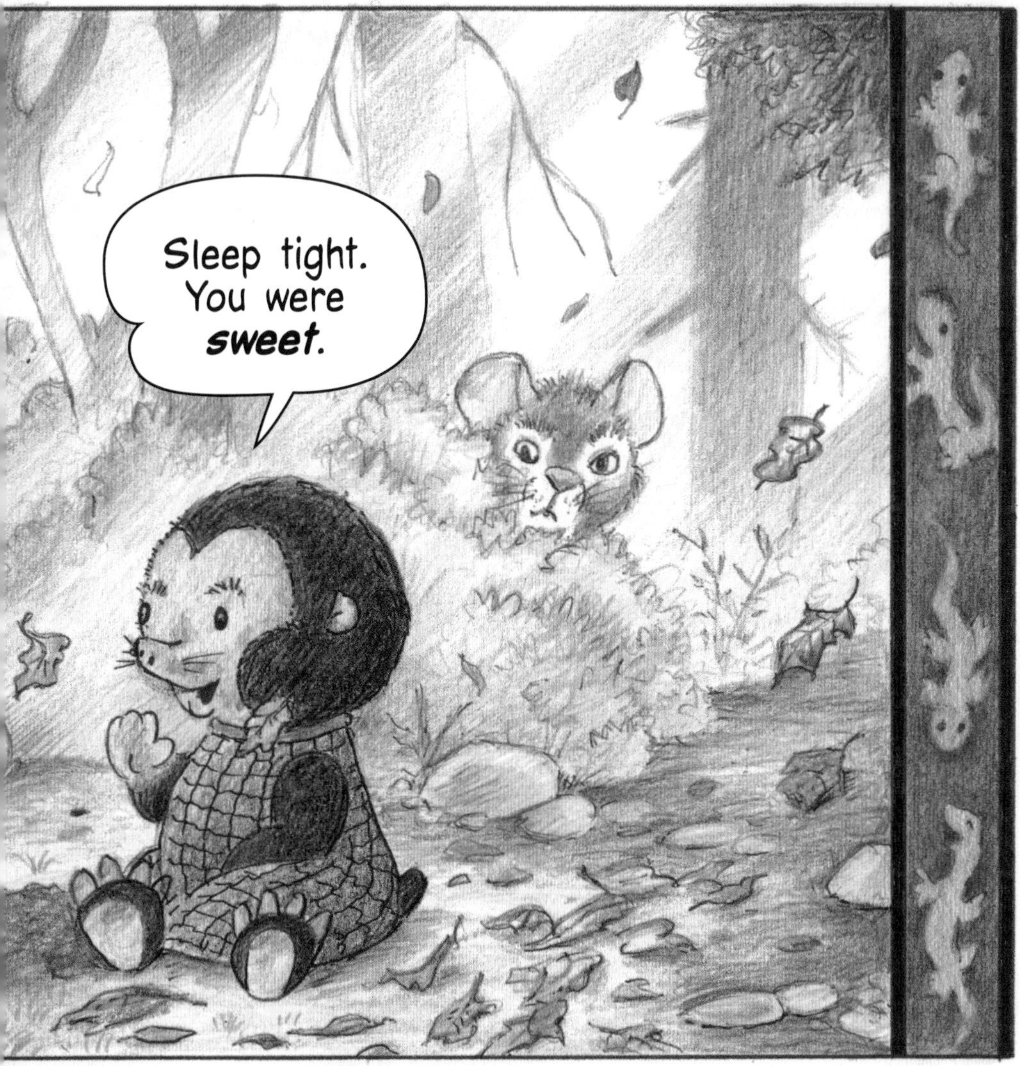
Sleep tight. You were ***sweet***.

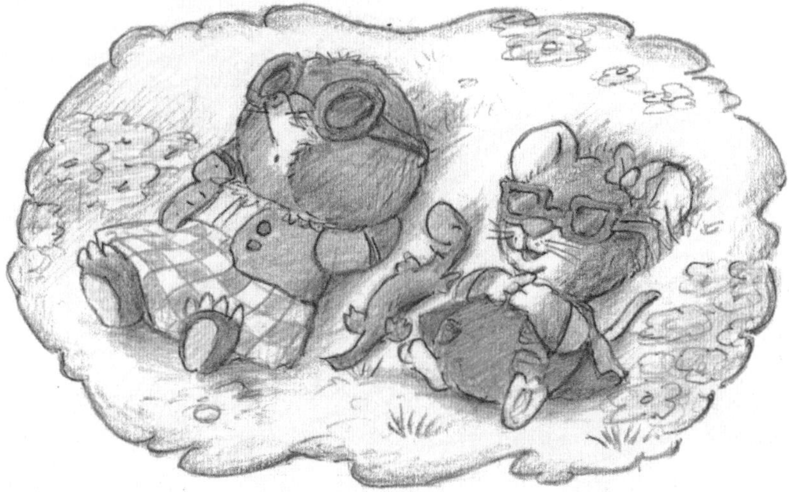

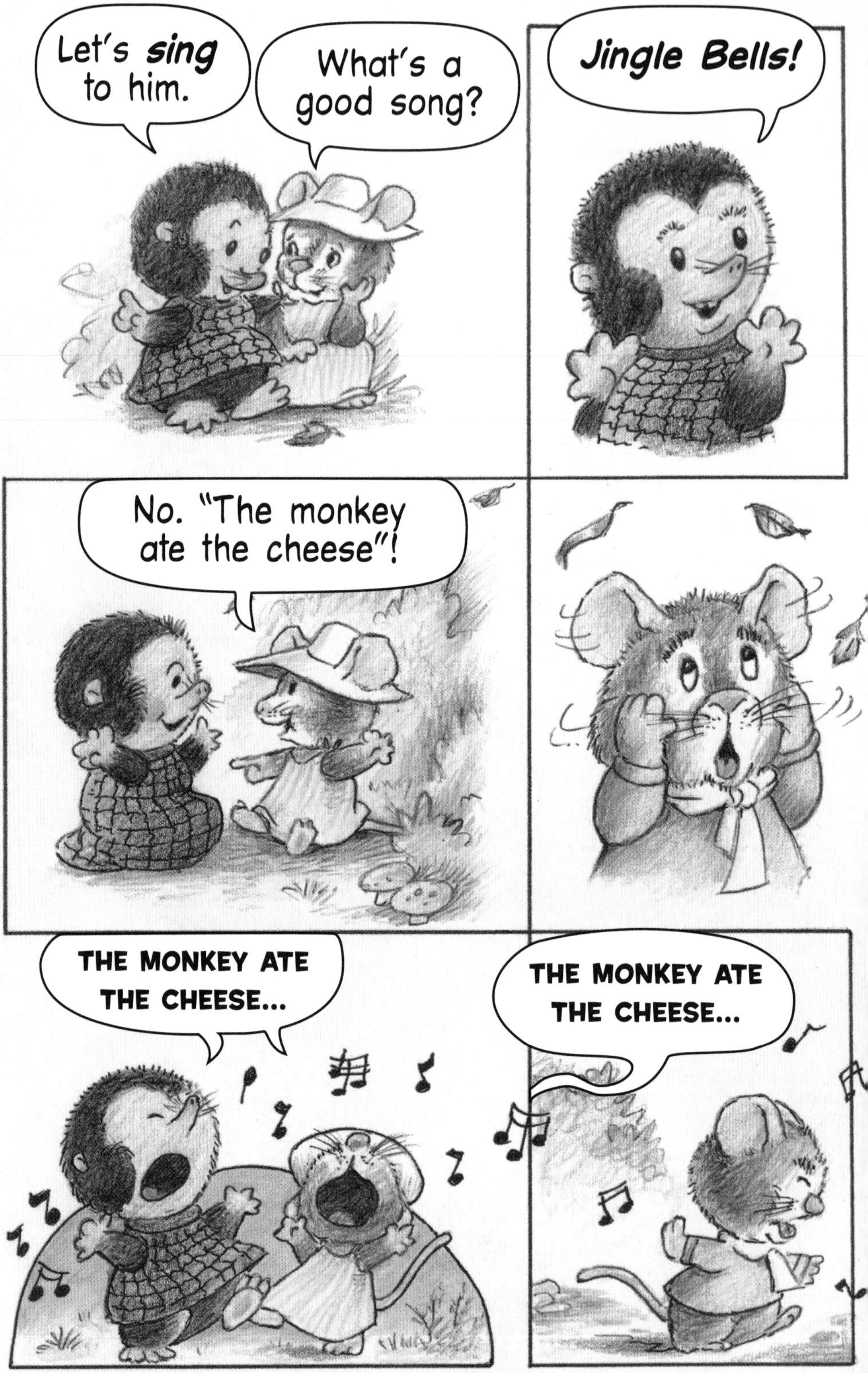
Let's *sing* to him.
What's a good song?
Jingle Bells!
No. "The monkey ate the cheese"!
THE MONKEY ATE THE CHEESE...
THE MONKEY ATE THE CHEESE...

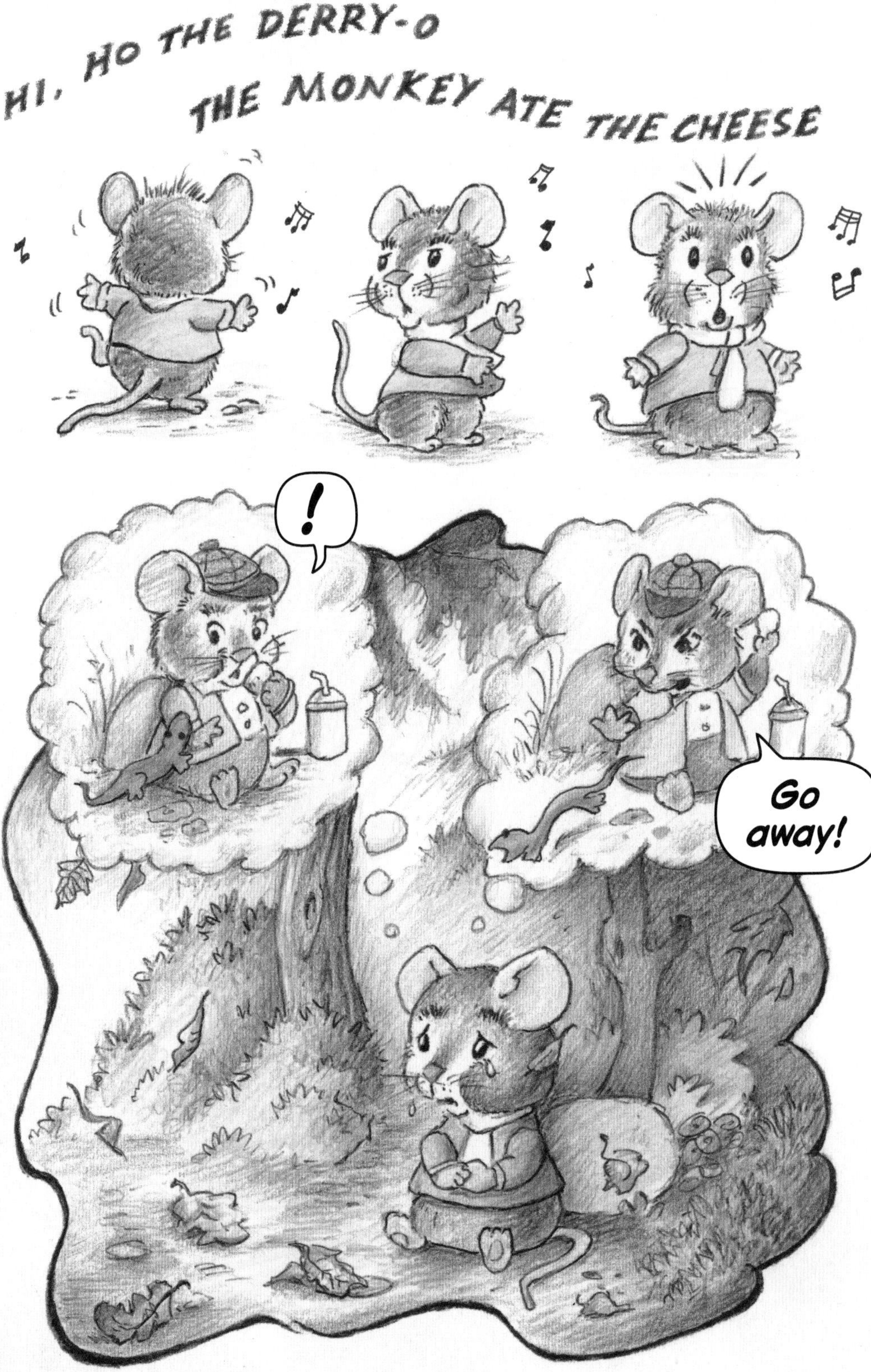
HI, HO THE DERRY-O
THE MONKEY ATE THE CHEESE
!
Go away!

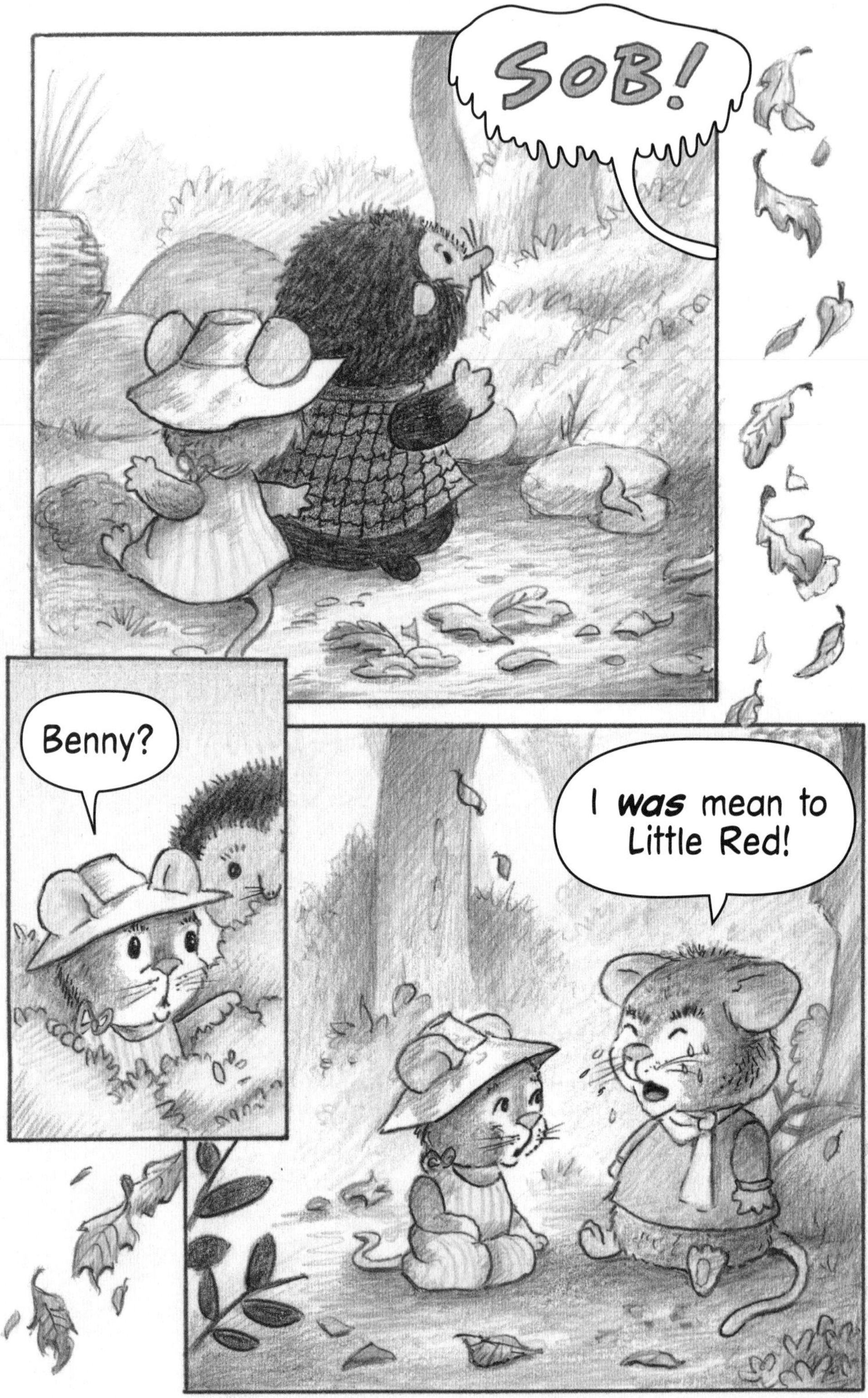
SOB!
Benny?
I *was* mean to Little Red!

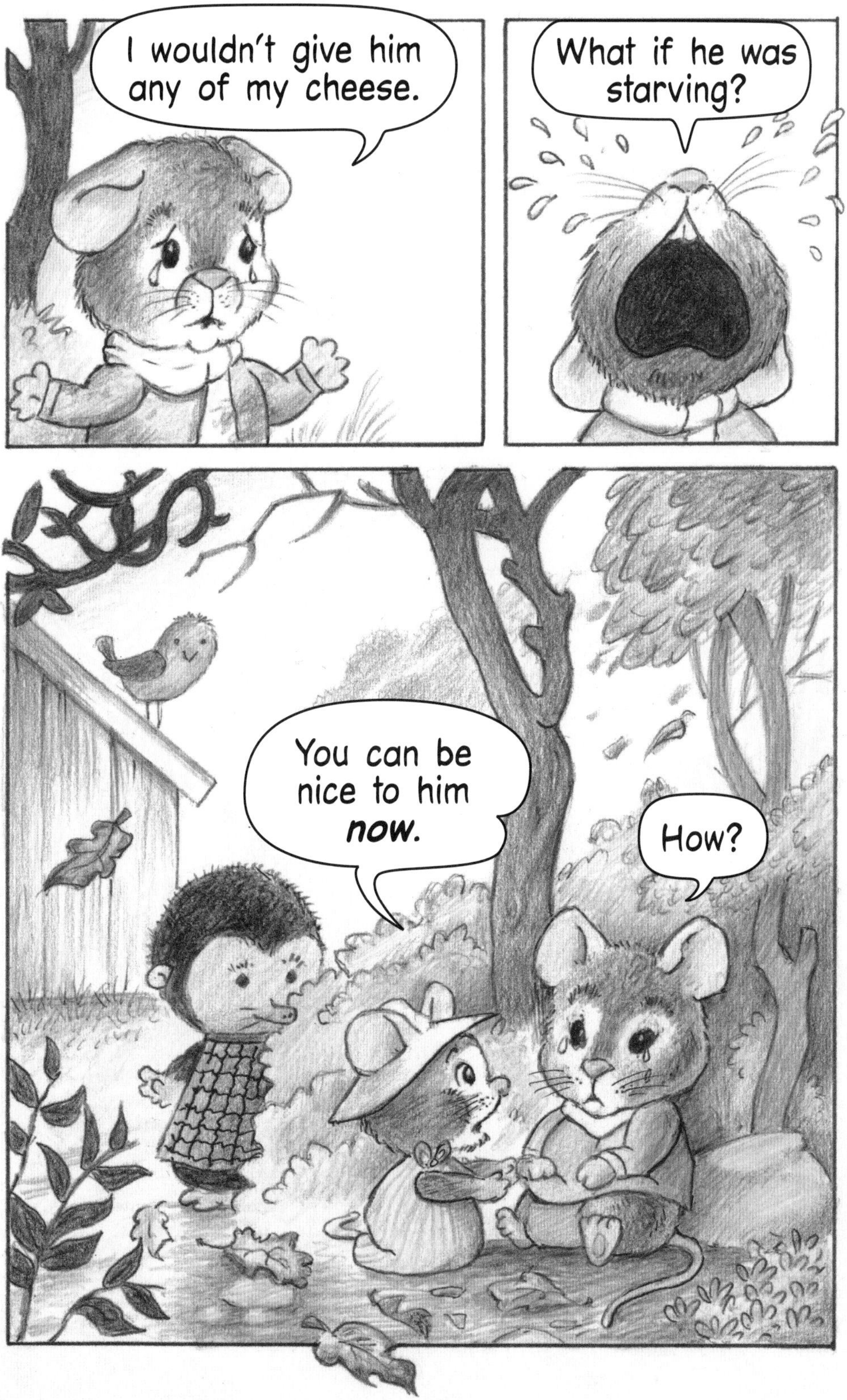
I wouldn't give him any of my cheese.
What if he was starving?
You can be nice to him *now*.
How?

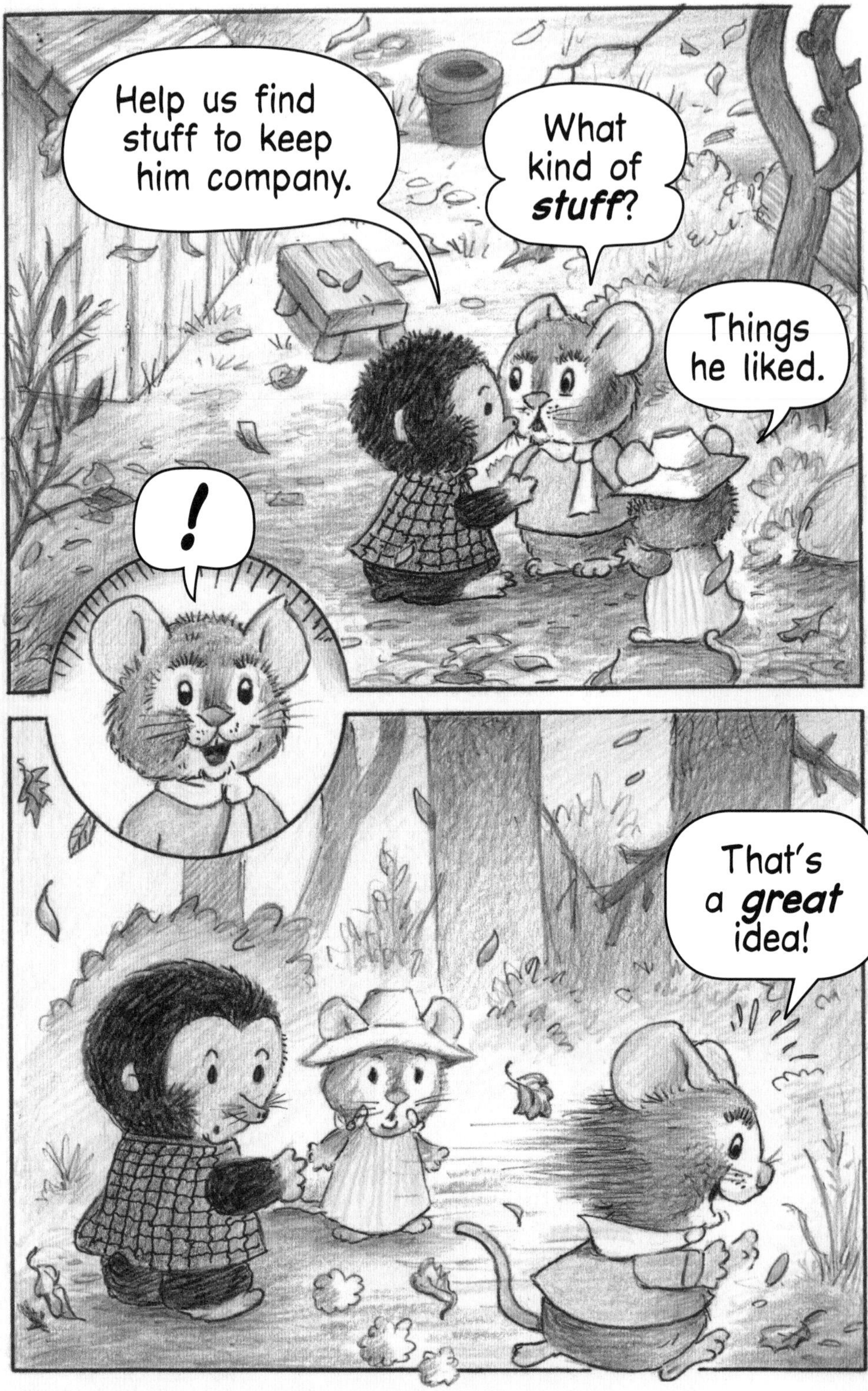
Help us find stuff to keep him company.
What kind of *stuff*?
Things he liked.
!
That's a *great* idea!

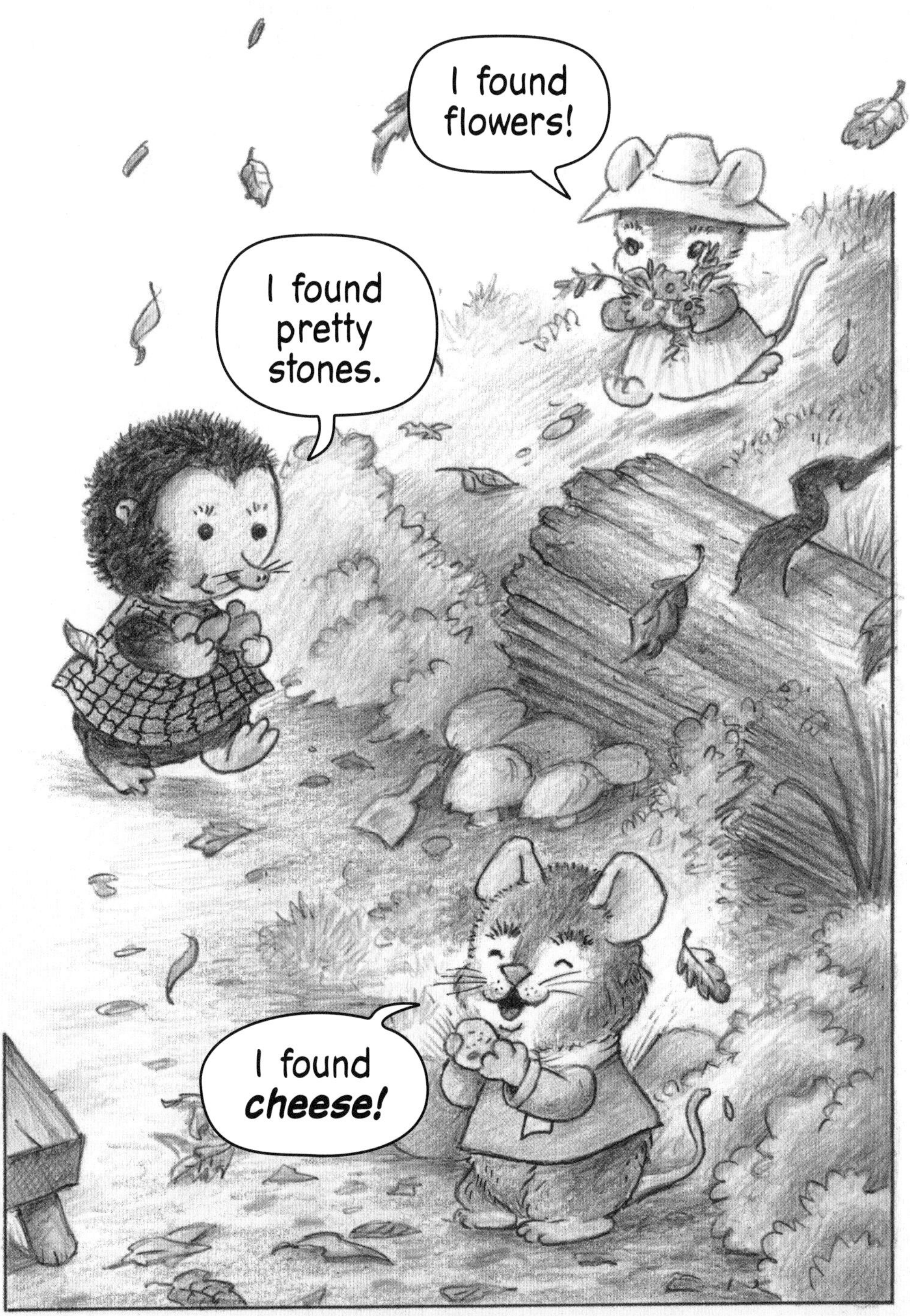
I found flowers!
I found pretty stones.
I found cheese!

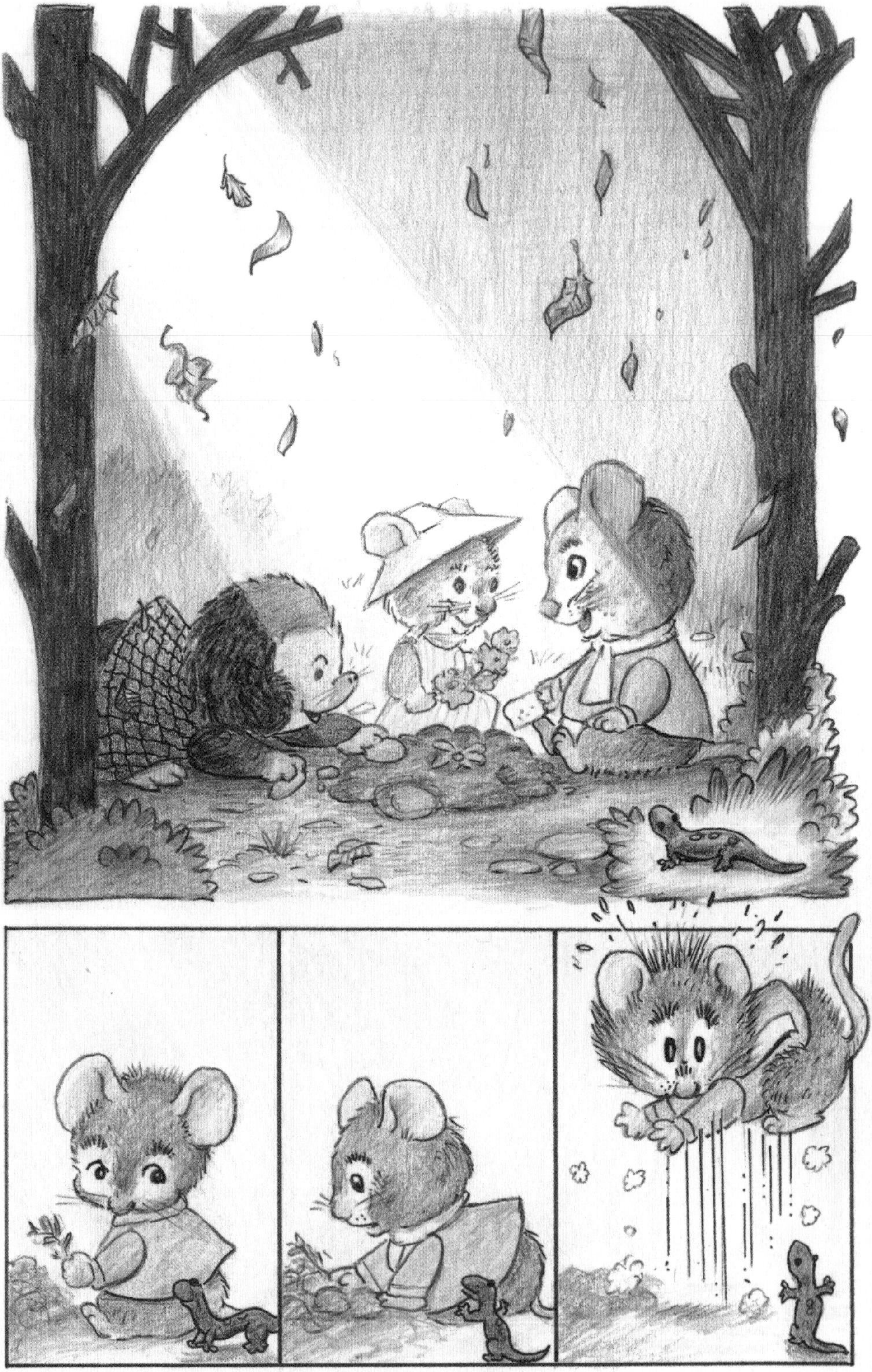

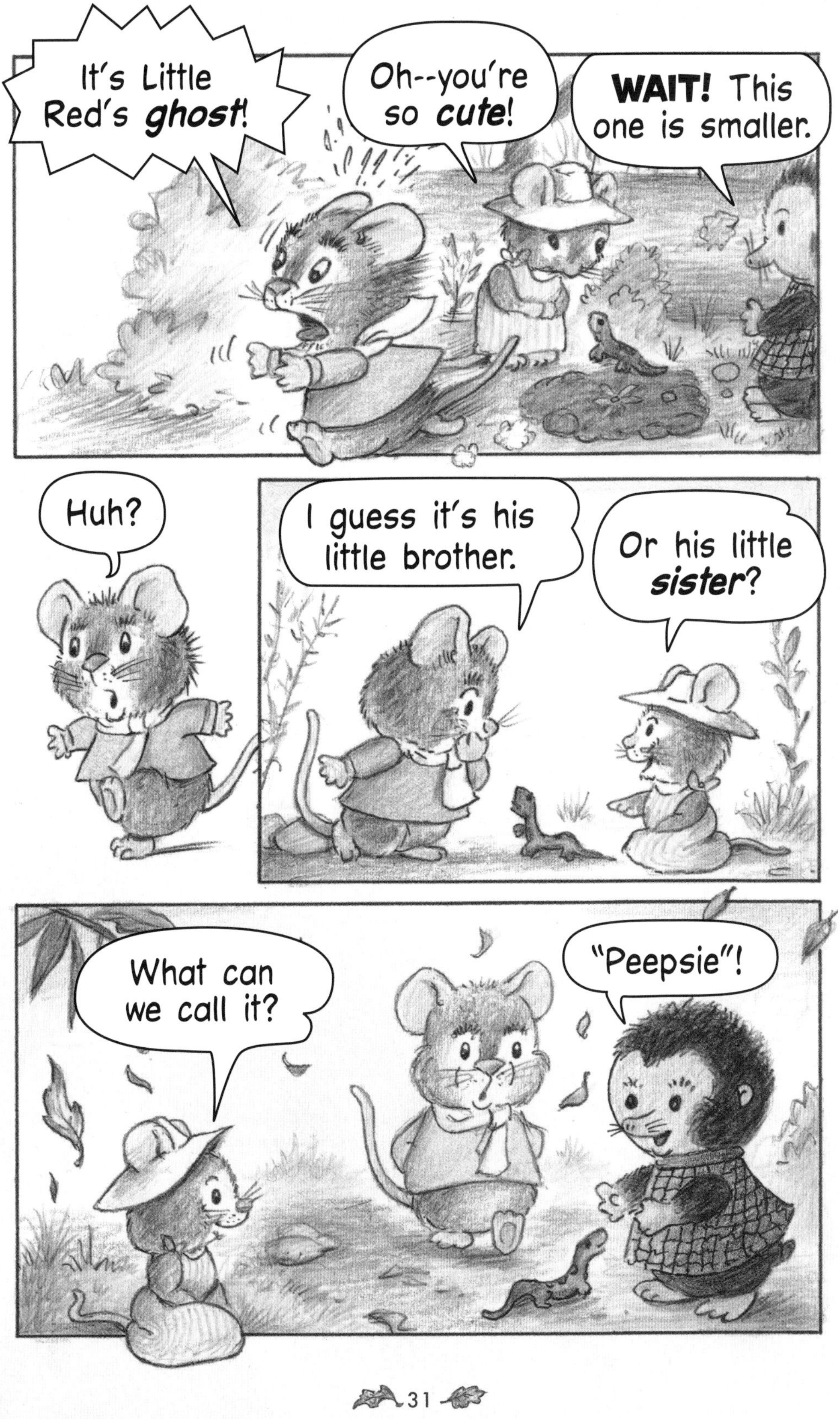
It's Little Red's *ghost*!
Oh--you're so *cute*!
WAIT! This one is smaller.
Huh?
I guess it's his little brother.
Or his little *sister*?
What can we call it?
"Peepsie"!

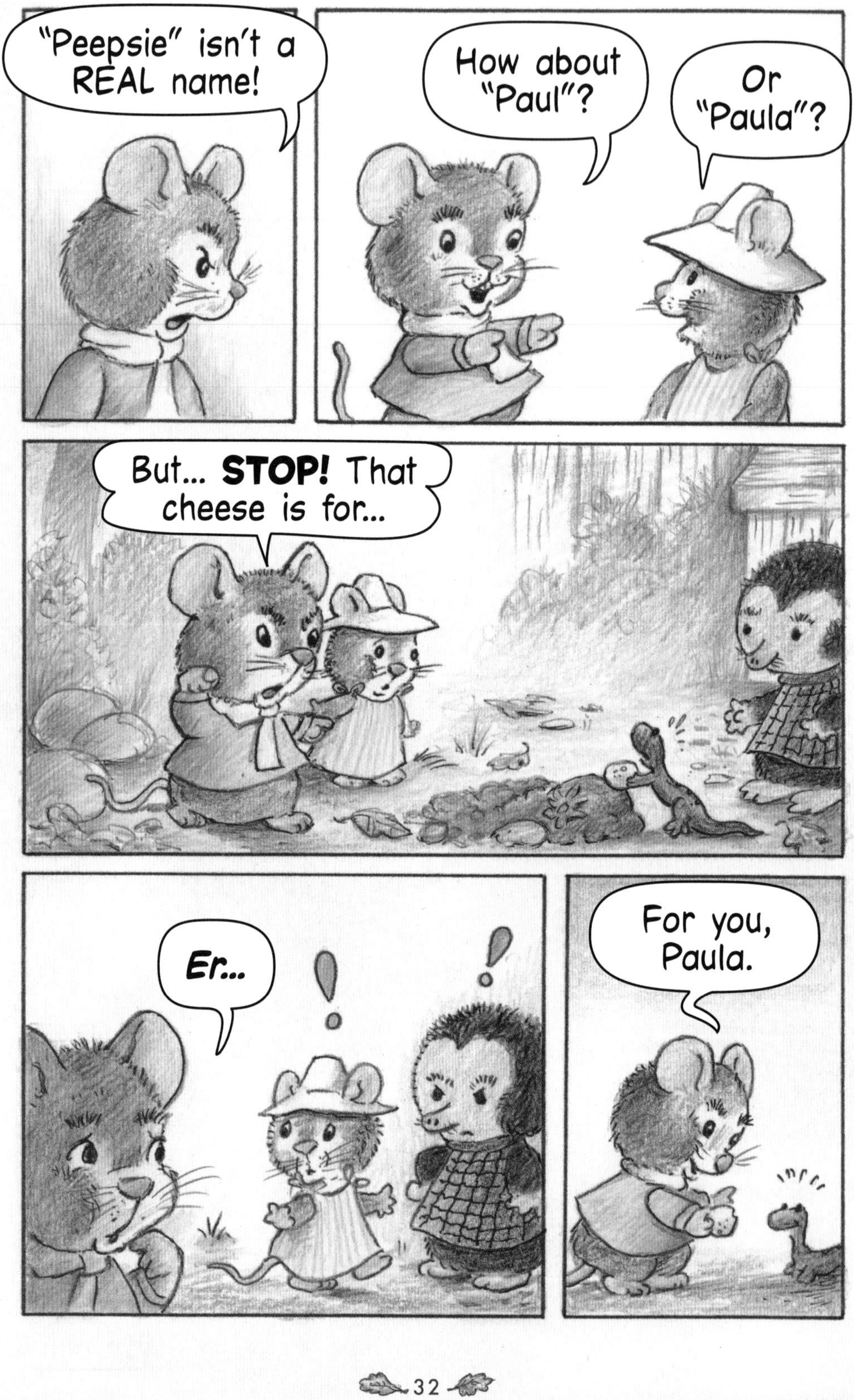
"Peepsie" isn't a REAL name!
How about "Paul"?
Or "Paula"?
But... **STOP!** That cheese is for...
Er...
For you, Paula.

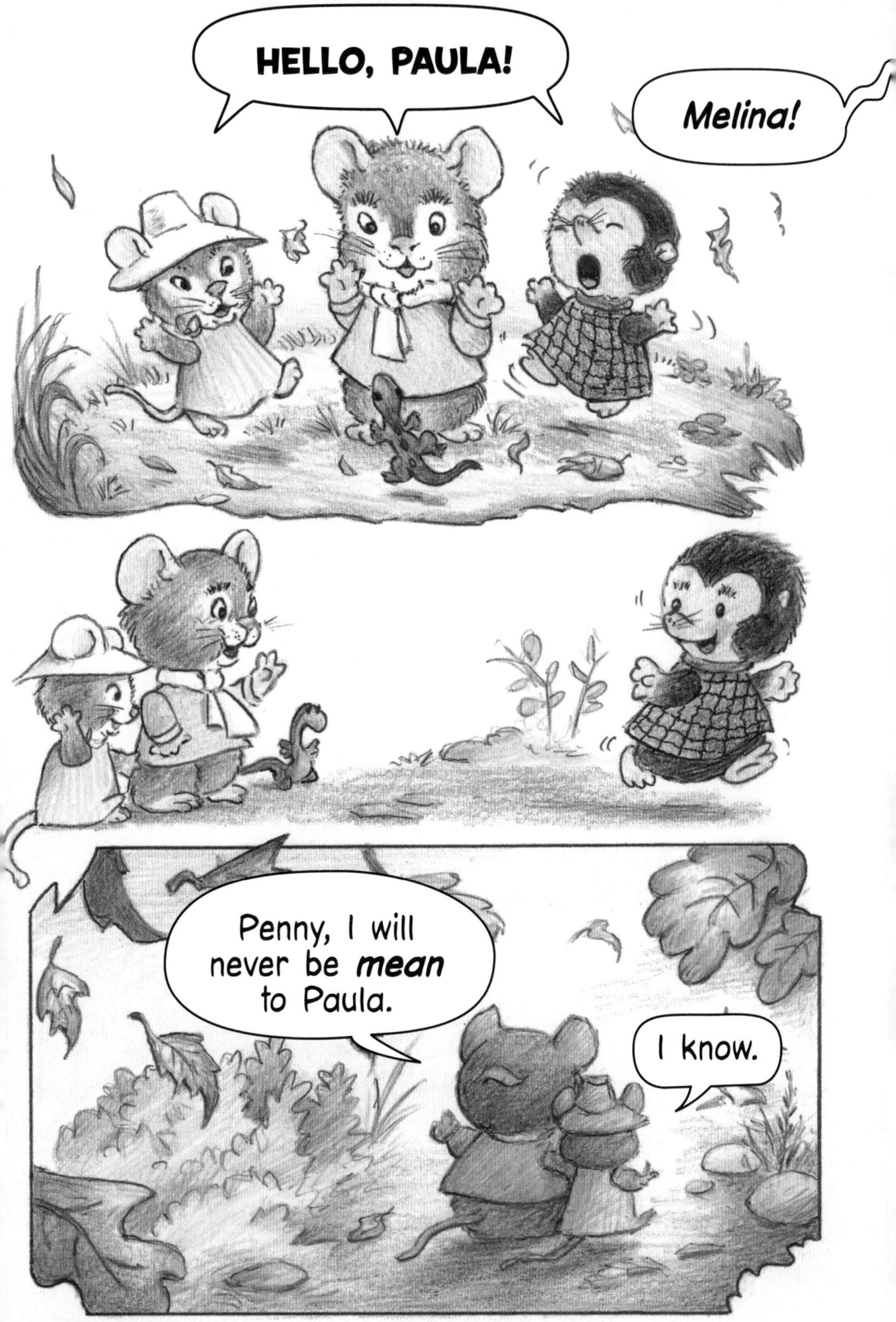
HELLO, PAULA!
Melina!
Penny, I will never be *mean* to Paula.
I know.

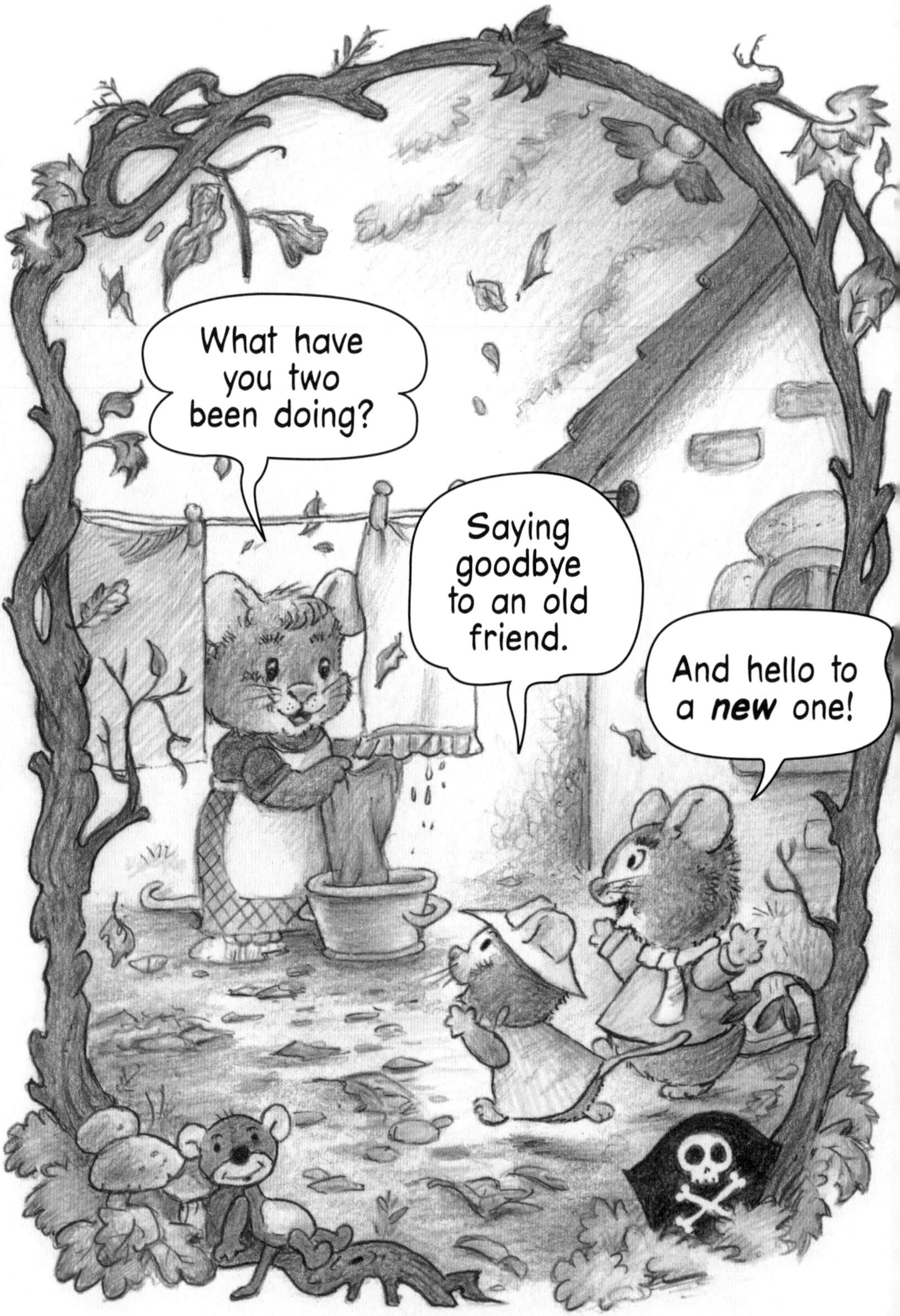
What have you two been doing?
Saying goodbye to an old friend.
And hello to a ***new*** one!

The Beginning

ABOUT THE AUTHOR

GEOFFREY HAYES has written and illustrated over forty children's books, including the extremely popular series of early readers *Otto and Uncle Tooth* and the classic *Bear by Himself.* His bestselling TOON Books series, Benny and Penny, has garnered multiple awards including the Theodor Seuss Geisel Award, given to a year's "most distinguished American book for beginning readers."

When Geoffrey and his brother were growing up in San Fransisco, they loved to look for crawling creatures in their backyard.

Geoffrey says, "Newts, geckos, and lizards are the most fun to draw–like little snakes with legs!"

COLLECT THEM ALL!

BENNY AND PENNY

BENNY AND PENNY
IN
JUST PRETEND
You can't play!
A TOON BOOK BY
GEOFFREY HAYES

BENNY AND PENNY
IN
THE BIG NO-NO!
Oh, Benny, this is a very big NO-NO!
Yes!
THEODOR SEUSS GEISEL AWARD
A TOON BOOK BY
GEOFFREY HAYES

THEODOR SEUSS GEISEL AWARD

BENNY AND PENNY
IN
THE TOY BREAKER
He is BACK!
Oh NO!
A TOON BOOK BY
GEOFFREY HAYES

BENNY AND PENNY
IN
LIGHTS OUT!
Benny, where are you GOING?
A TOON BOOK BY
GEOFFREY HAYES

BENNY AND PENNY
IN
LOST AND FOUND!
Benny, I want to go home!
ME TOO!
A TOON BOOK BY
GEOFFREY HAYES

BENNY AND PENNY
IN
HOW TO SAY GOODBYE
PENNY- What happened?
Sniff-
A TOON BOOK BY
GEOFFREY HAYES

Named
Best Continuing
Series for
Beginning Readers
by Kirkus Reviews.

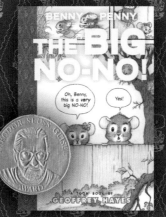

TIPS FOR PARENTS AND TEACHERS:
HOW TO READ COMICS WITH KIDS

Kids **love** comics! They are naturally drawn to the details in the pictures, which make them want to read the words. Comics beg for repeated readings and let both emerging and reluctant readers enjoy complex stories with a rich vocabulary. But since comics have their own grammar, here are a few tips for reading them with kids:

GUIDE YOUNG READERS: Use your finger to show your place in the text, but keep it at the bottom of the speaking character so it doesn't hide the very important facial expressions.

HAM IT UP! Think of the comic book story as a play and don't hesitate to read with expression and intonation. Assign parts or get kids to supply the sound effects, a great way to reinforce phonics skills.

LET THEM GUESS. Comics provide lots of context for the words, so emerging readers can make informed guesses. Like jigsaw puzzles, comics ask readers to make connections, so check a young audience's understanding by asking "What's this character thinking?" (but don't be surprised if a kid finds some of the comics' subtle details faster than you).

TALK ABOUT THE PICTURES. Point out how the artist paces the story with pauses (silent panels) or speeded-up action (a burst of short panels). Discuss how the size and shape of the panels convey meaning.

ABOVE ALL, ENJOY! There is of course never one right way to read, so go for the shared pleasure. Once children make the story happen in their imaginations, they have discovered the thrill of reading, and you won't be able to stop them. At that point, just go get them more books, and more comics.

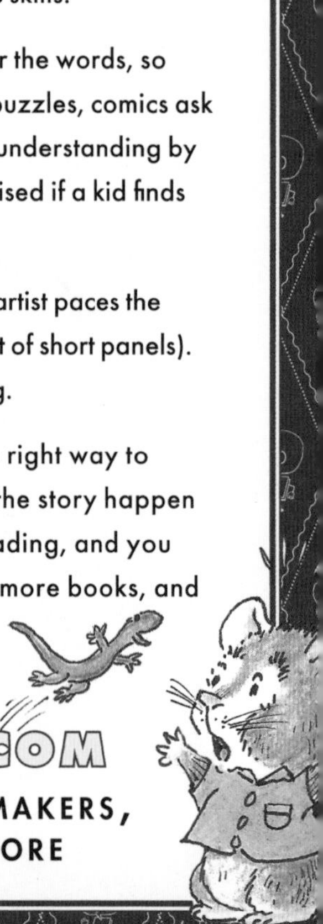

TOON-BOOKS.COM
SEE OUR FREE ONLINE CARTOON MAKERS, LESSON PLANS, AND MUCH MORE

Dear Parent:
Your child's love of reading starts here!

Every child learns to read in a different way and at his or her own speed. Some go back and forth between reading levels and read favorite books again and again. Others read through each level in order. You can help your young reader improve and become more confident by encouraging his or her own interests and abilities. From books your child reads with you to the first books he or she reads alone, there are I Can Read Books for every stage of reading:

SHARED READING
Basic language, word repetition, and whimsical illustrations, ideal for sharing with your emergent reader

BEGINNING READING
Short sentences, familiar words, and simple concepts for children eager to read on their own

READING WITH HELP
Engaging stories, longer sentences, and language play for developing readers

READING ALONE
Complex plots, challenging vocabulary, and high-interest topics for the independent reader

ADVANCED READING
Short paragraphs, chapters, and exciting themes for the perfect bridge to chapter books

I Can Read Books have introduced children to the joy of reading since 1957. Featuring award-winning authors and illustrators and a fabulous cast of beloved characters, I Can Read Books set the standard for beginning readers.

A lifetime of discovery begins with the magical words **"I Can Read!"**

Visit www.icanread.com for information
on enriching your child's reading experience.

For stargazers everywhere
—J.O'C.

For Yarden and Yonatan,
who shine brightly in my heart
—R.P.G.

For the PA Stargazers,
whose friendship bends the Space/Time Continuum
—T.E.

HarperCollins®, ■®, and I Can Read Book® are trademarks of HarperCollins Publishers.
Fancy Nancy Sees Stars Text copyright © 2008 by Jane O'Connor Illustrations copyright © 2008 by Robin Preiss Glasser
All rights reserved. Printed in the United States of America. No part of this book may be used or reproduced in any manner what-
soever without written permission except in the case of brief quotations embodied in critical articles and reviews. For information
address HarperCollins Children's Books, a division of HarperCollins Publishers, 10 East 53rd Street, New York, NY 10022.

www.icanread.com

Library of Congress Cataloging-in-Publication Data
O'Connor, Jane.
    Fancy Nancy sees stars / by Jane O'Connor ; cover illustration by Robin Preiss Glasser ; interior illustrations by Ted Enik. —
1st ed.
        p.   cm. — (I can read book) (Fancy Nancy)
    Summary: When a rainstorm prevents Nancy and her friend Robert from getting to the planetarium the night of a class field trip,
she has a brilliant idea for making things better.
    ISBN 978-0-06-123611-2 (pbk.) — ISBN 978-0-06-123612-9 (trade bdg.)
    [1. Astronomy—Fiction.   2. School field trips—Fiction.   3. Planetariums—Fiction.]   I. Enik, Ted, ill.   II. Title.
PZ7.O222Fgs   2009   2008010284
[E]—dc22   CIP
                                                                                                                                                                    AC

                    10 11 12 13 14   LP/WOR   10 9   ❖   First Edition

I Can Read! BEGINNING 1 READING

Fancy Nancy Sees Stars

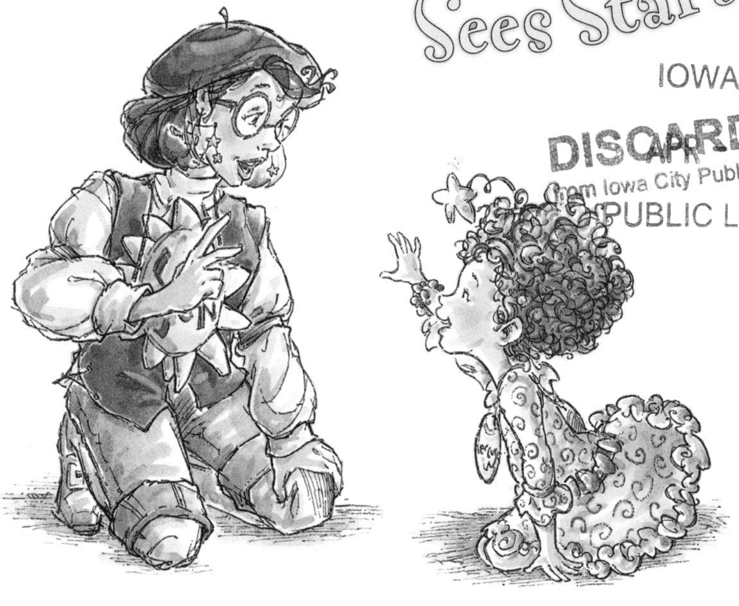

by Jane O'Connor

cover illustration by Robin Preiss Glasser

interior illustrations by Ted Enik

HarperCollins*Publishers*

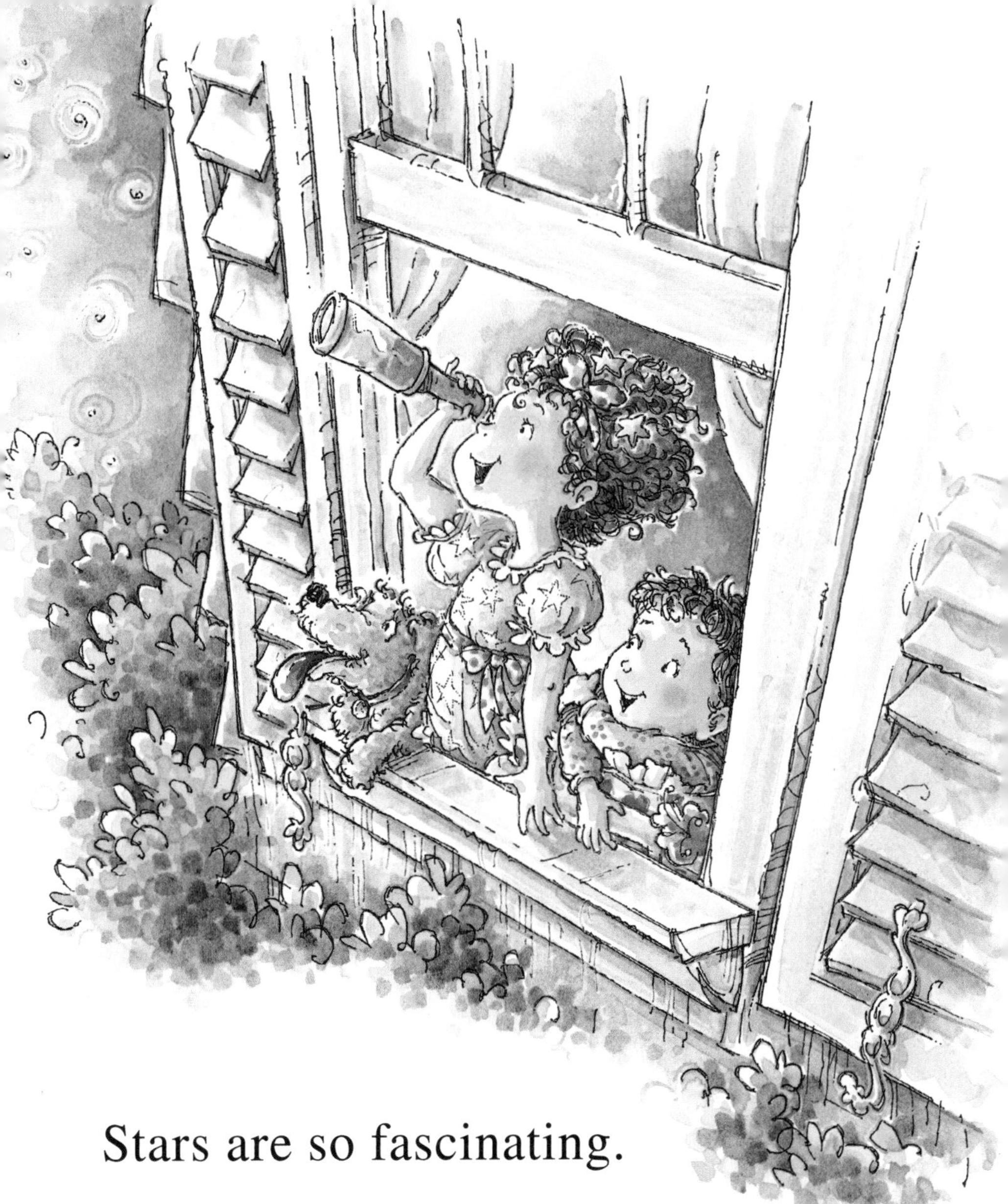

Stars are so fascinating.

(That's a fancy word

for interesting.)

I love how they sparkle in the sky.

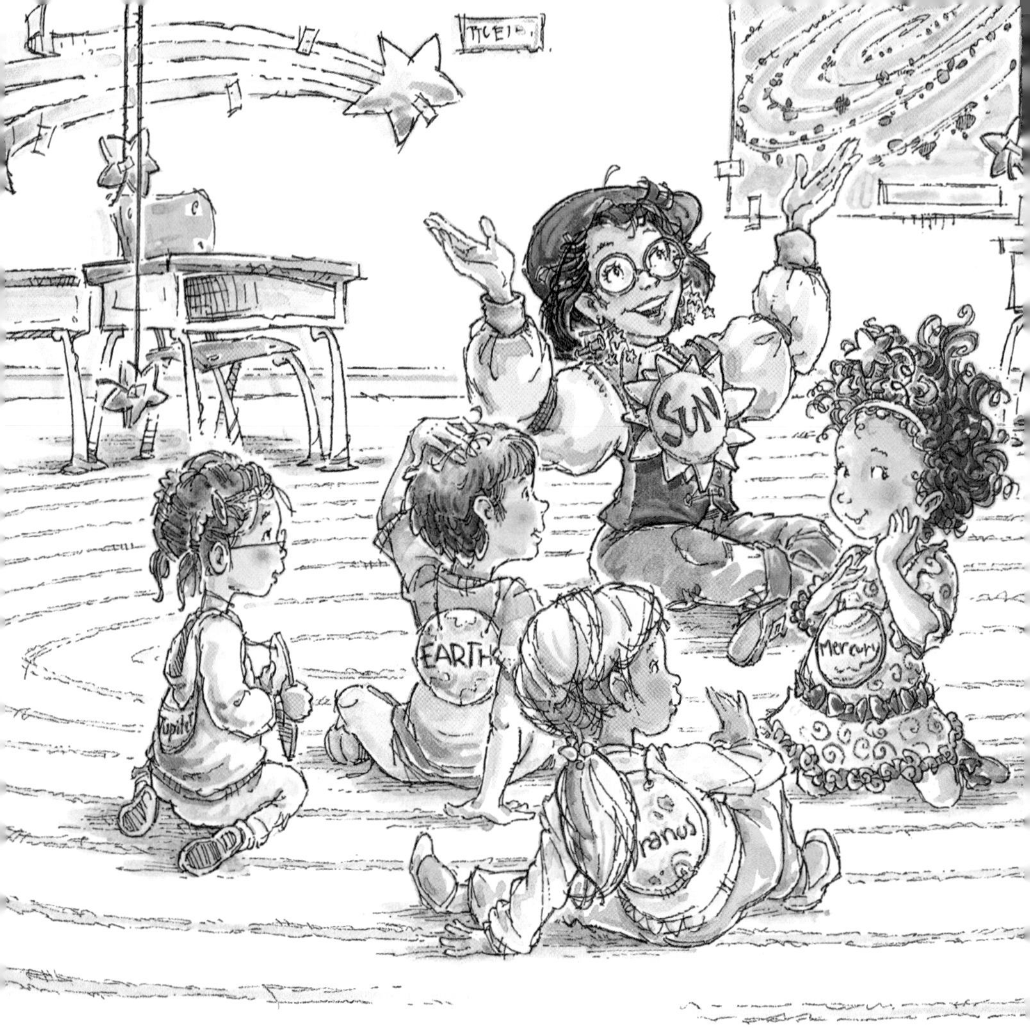
SUN
EARTH
Mercury

Tonight is our class trip.

Yes! It's a class trip at night!

We are going to the planetarium.

That is a museum

about stars and planets.

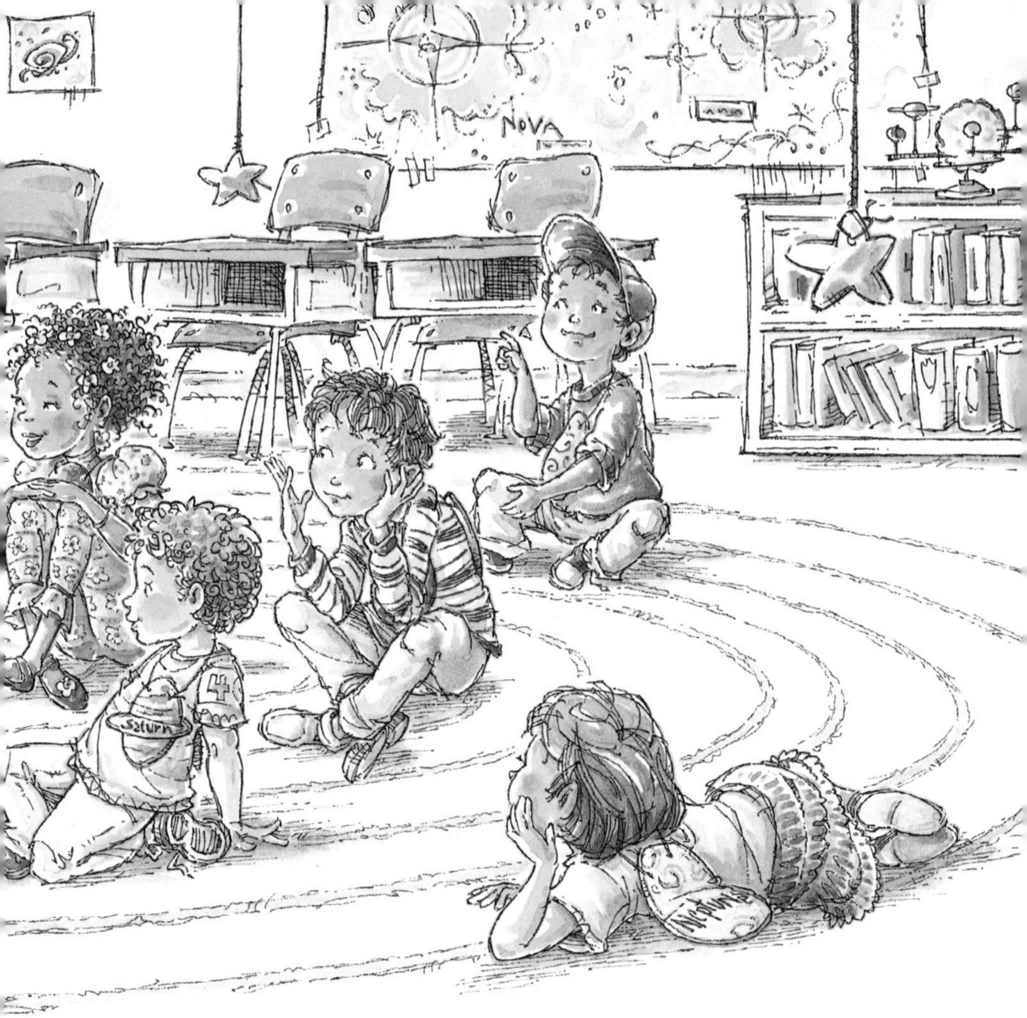
NOVA
Saturn

Ms. Glass tells us,

"The show starts at eight.

We will all meet there."

I smile at my friend Robert.

My parents are taking Robert and me.

Then Ms. Glass asks,

“What star is closest to Earth?”

That’s easy.

It’s the sun.

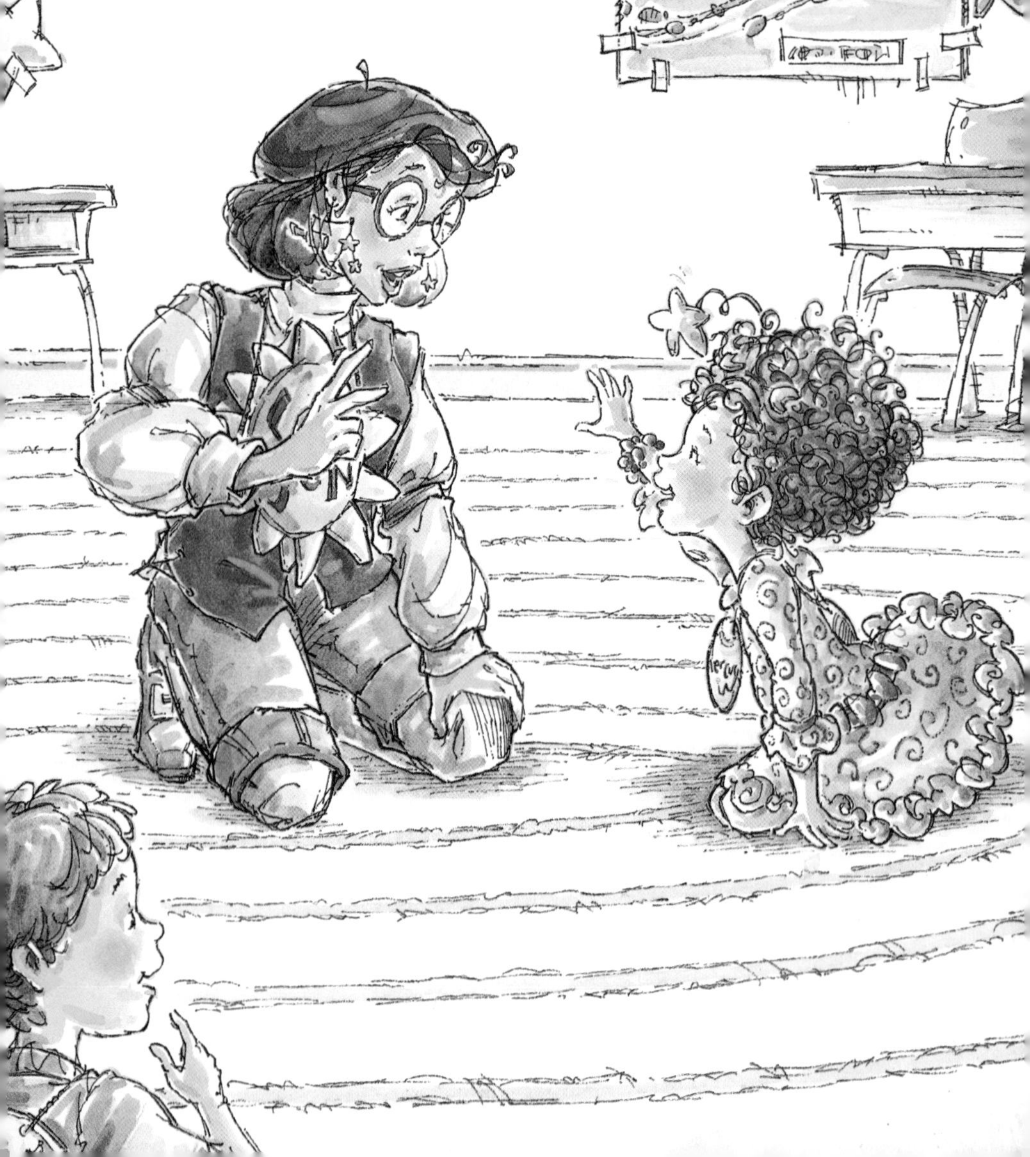

“What do you call stars
that make a picture?”
asks Ms. Glass.
Robert and Bree have both forgotten.
“I know, I know,” I say.
“A constellation.”

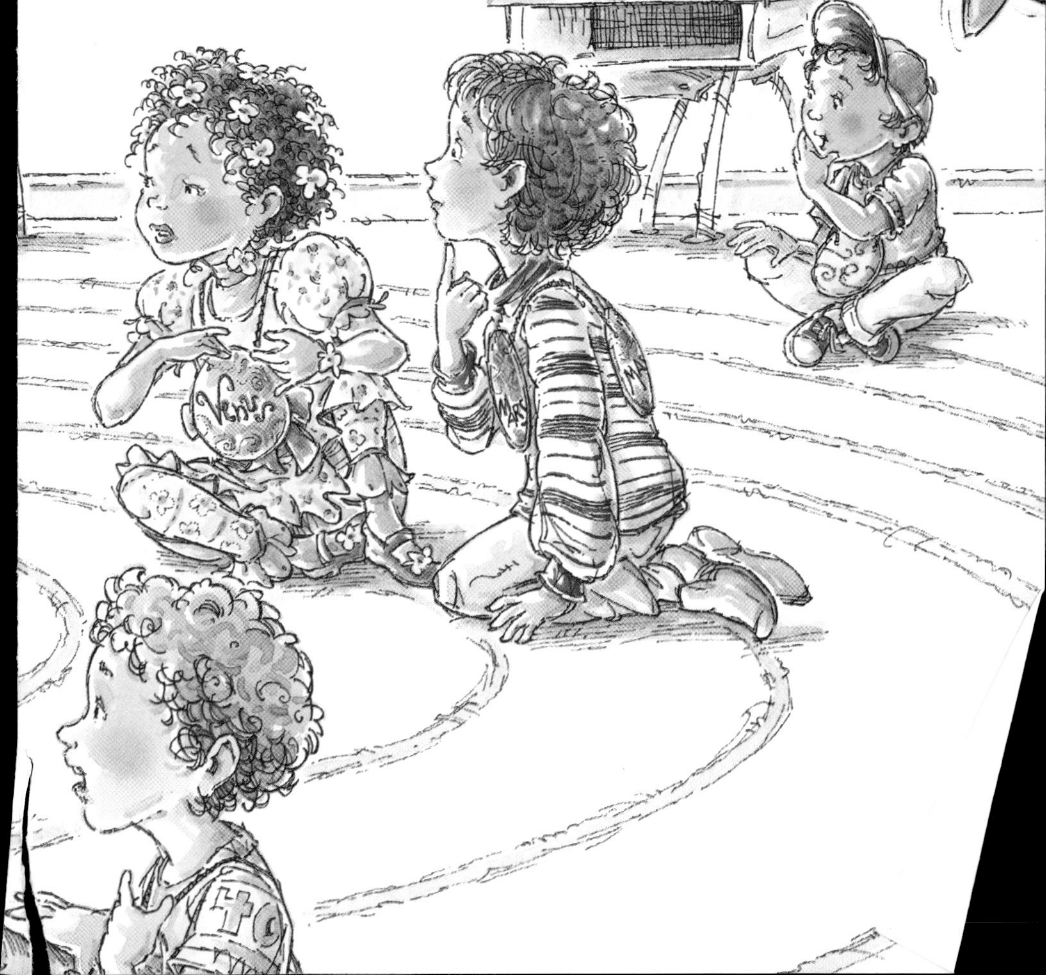

Ms. Glass nods.

On the wall are pictures.

There's the hunter and the crab

and the Big Dipper.

It looks like a big spoon.

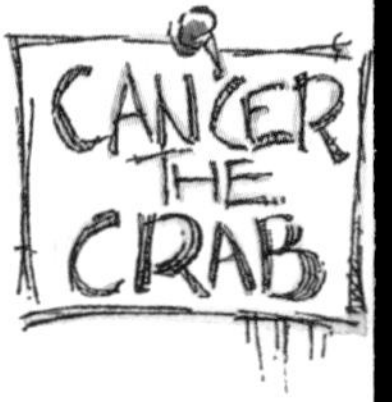
CANCER THE CRAB

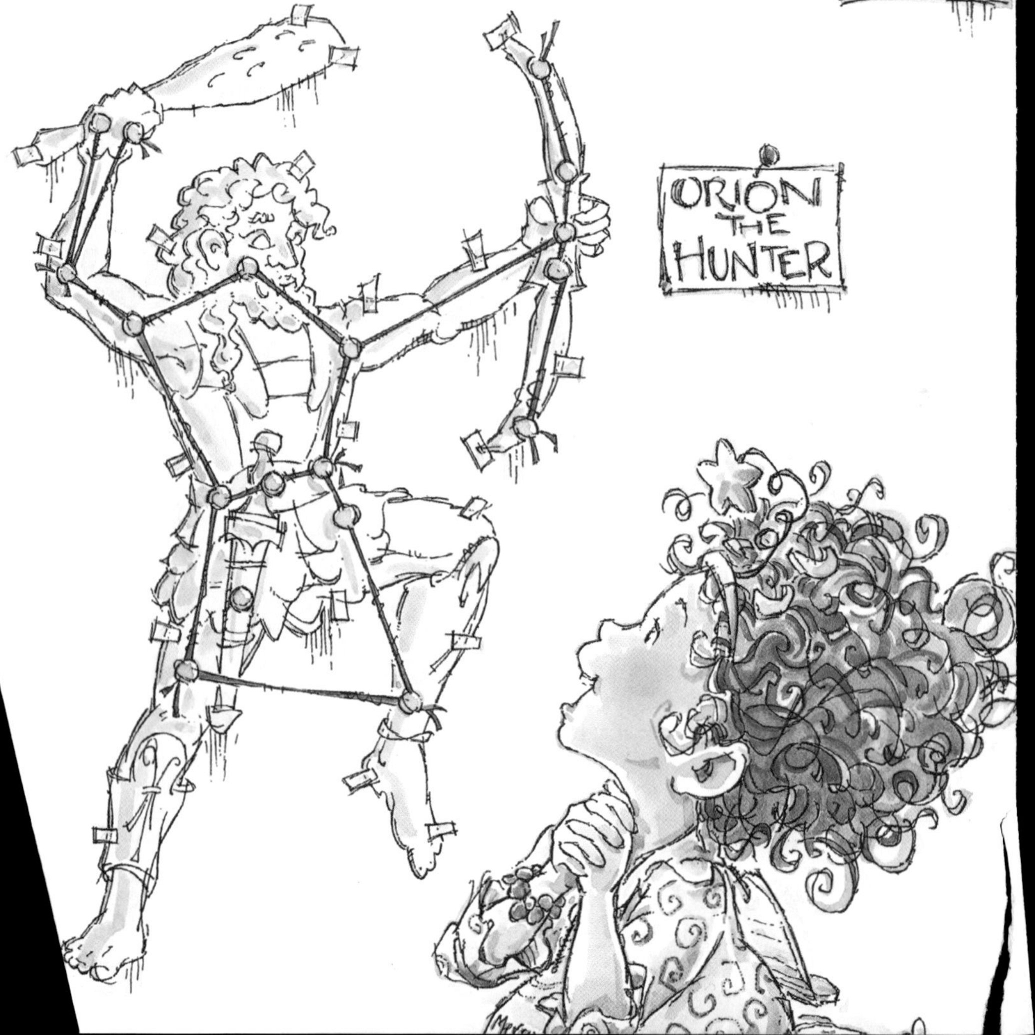
ORION THE HUNTER

We will see all of them at the show.

I can hardly wait.

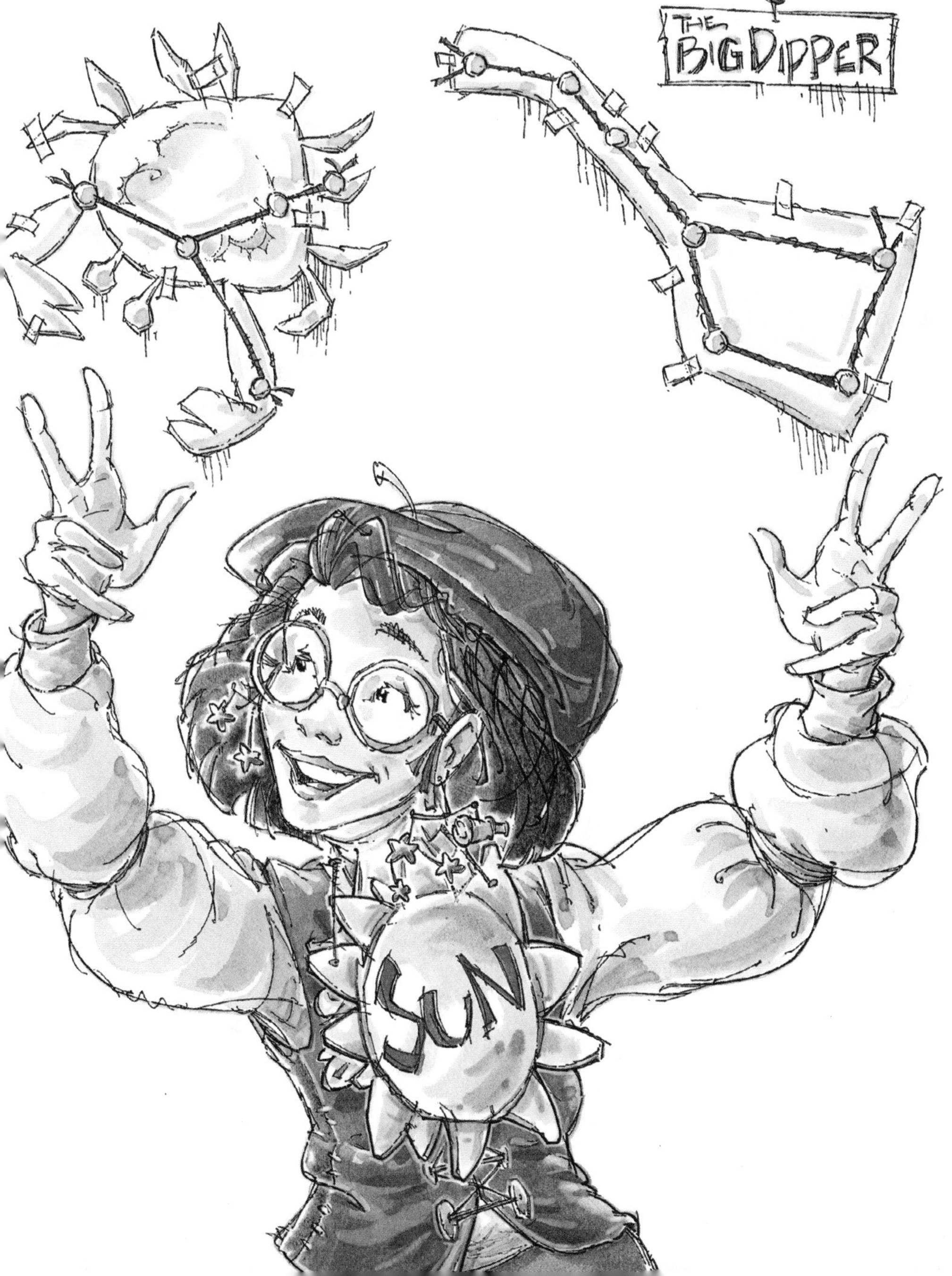
THE BIG DIPPER
SUN

At home, Robert and I
put glow-in-the-dark stickers
on our T-shirts.
Mine has the Big Dipper.
Robert has the hunter on his.

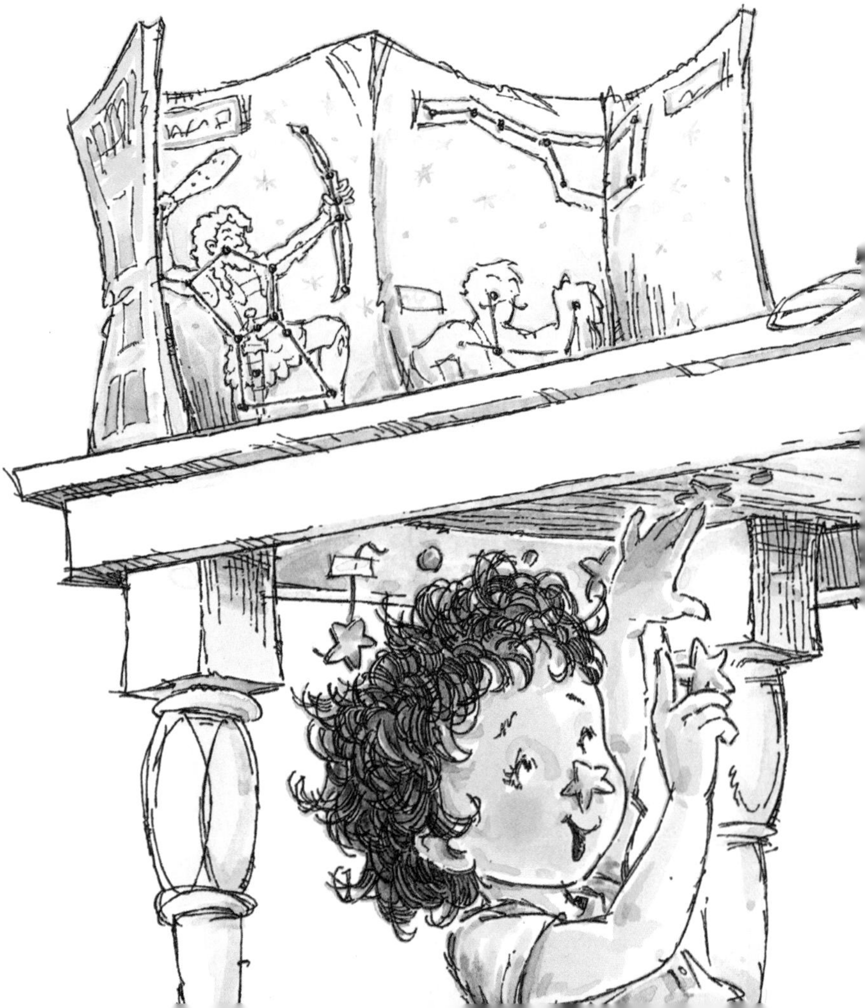

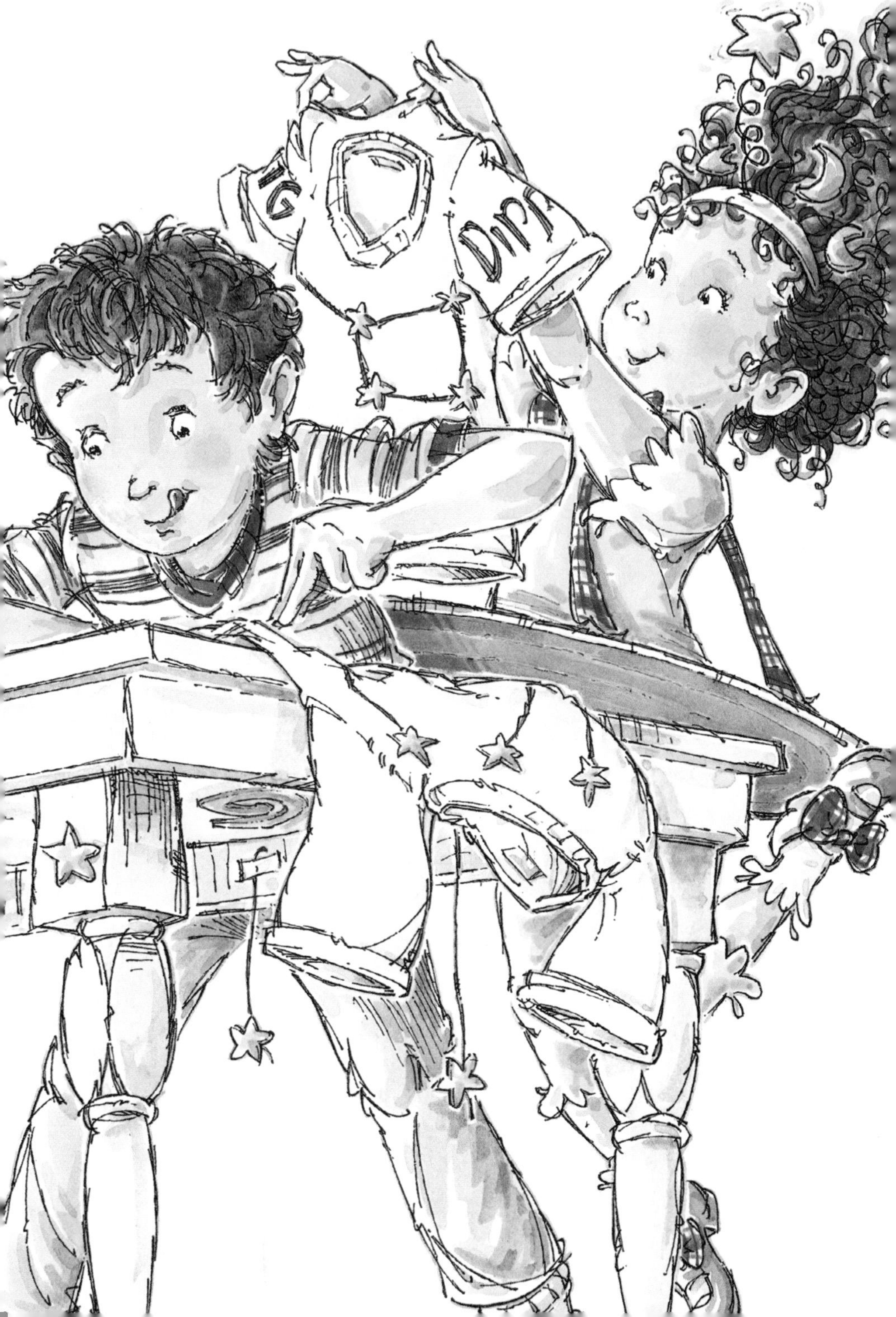

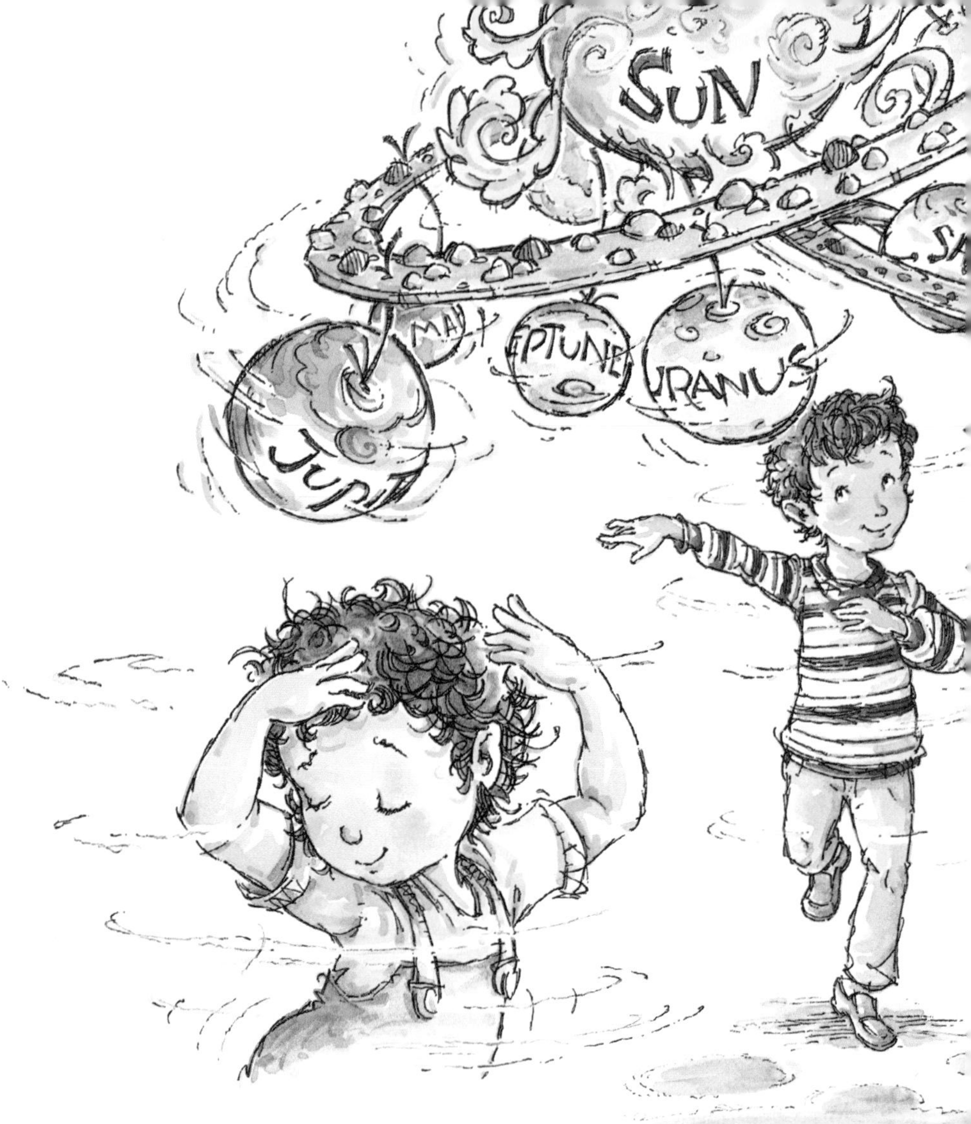
SUN

We spin my mobile
and watch the planets orbit the sun.
(Orbit is a fancy word.
It means to travel in a circle.)

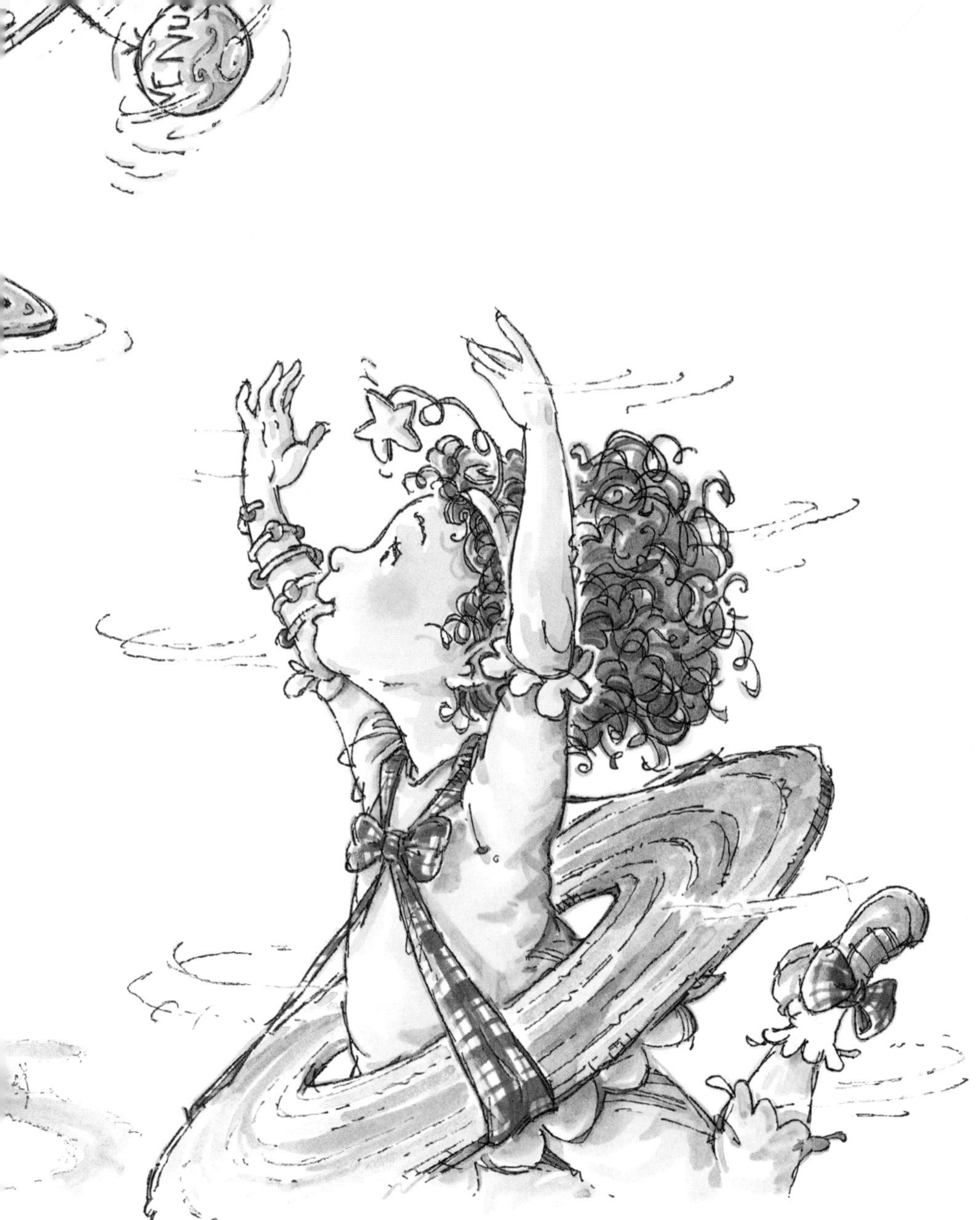

Then we pretend to orbit
until we get dizzy.

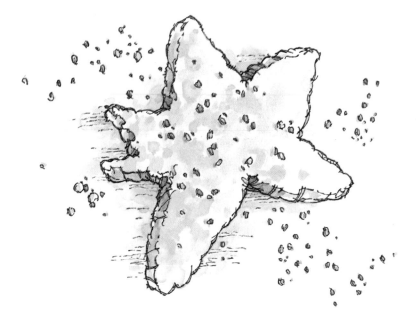

Later, we bake star cookies.

Sprinkles make them sparkle.

"The sun is a star,"

I tell my sister.

"It is the closest star,

so we see it in the day."

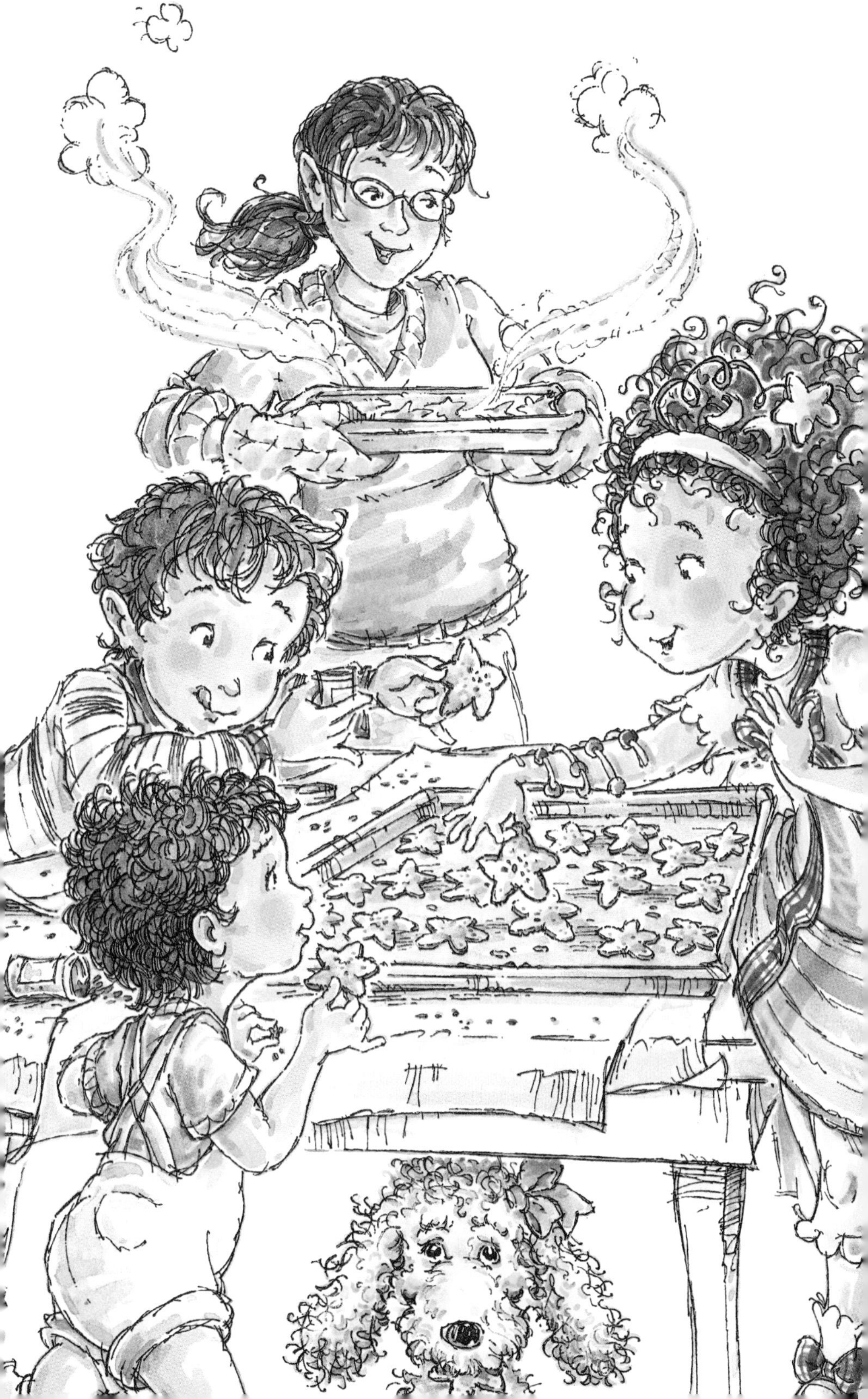

After dinner,

we wait for the baby-sitter.

She is very late.

Dad says not to worry.

We have plenty of time.

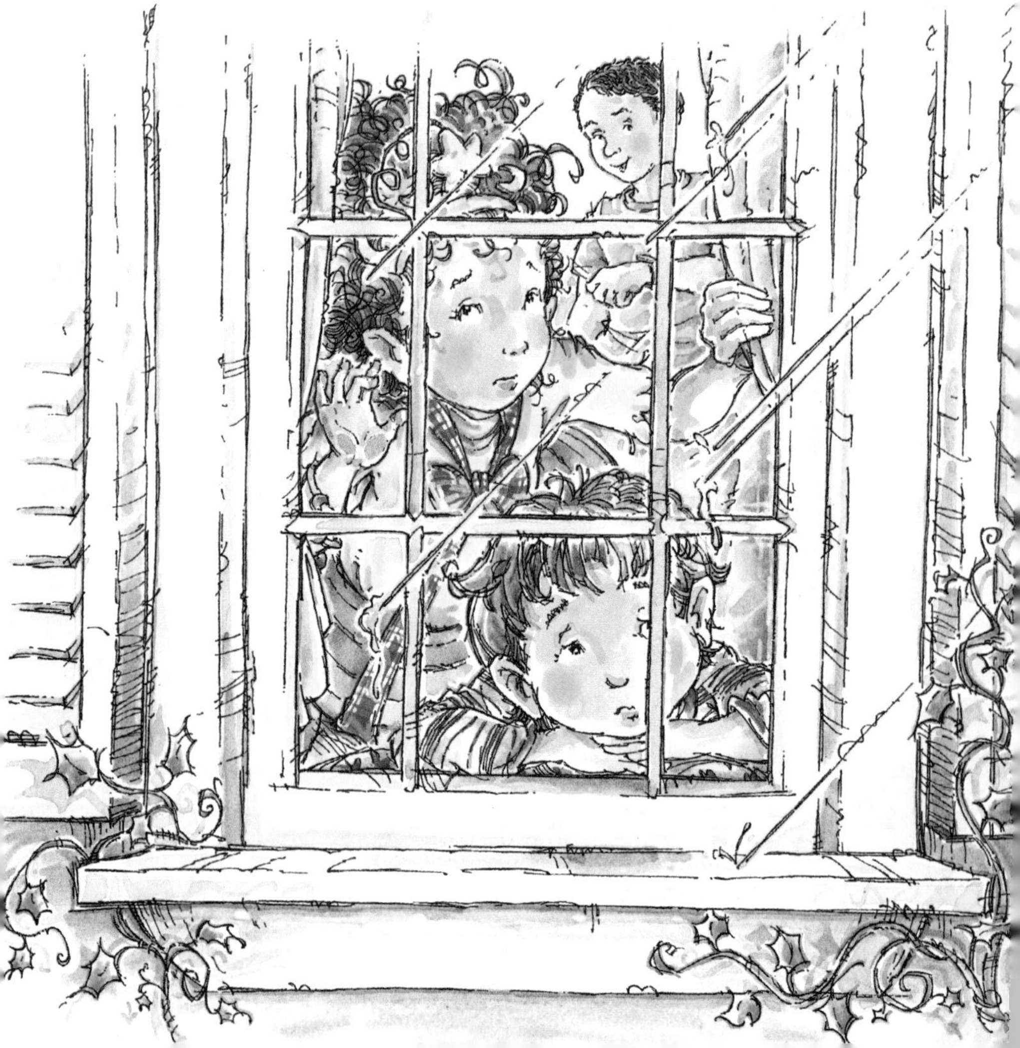

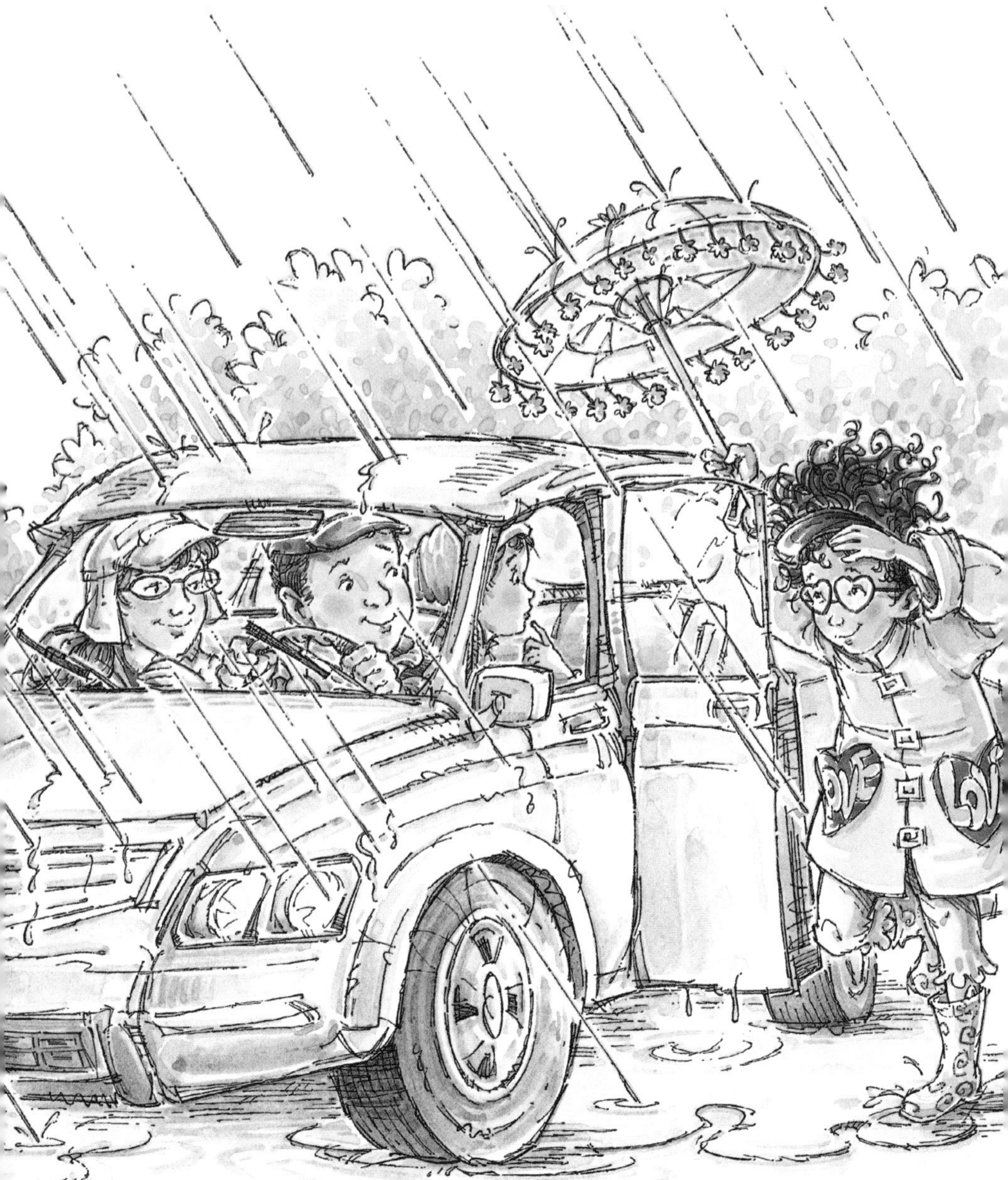
LOVE
LOVE

At last we get in the car.

Drip, drip, drip.

It is raining.

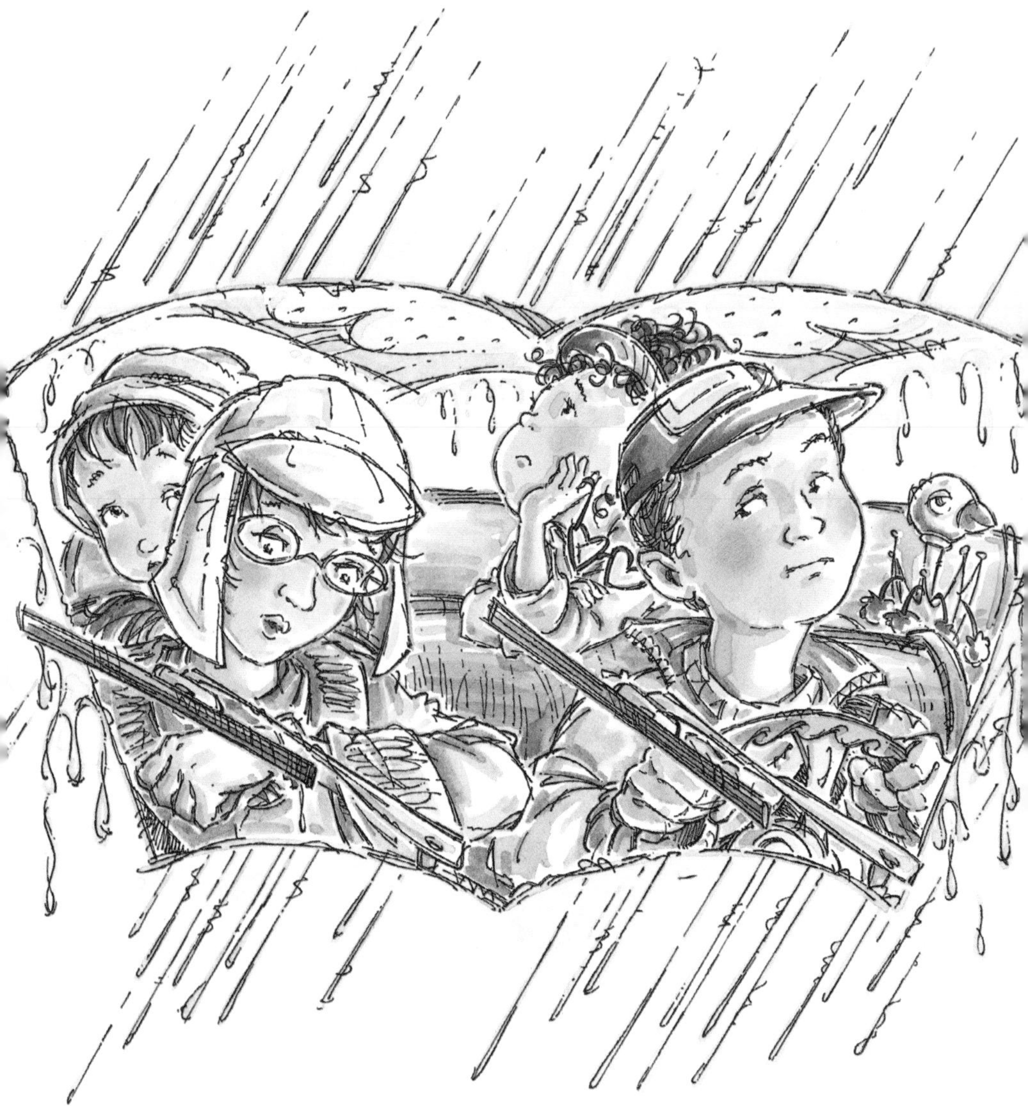

The rain comes down
harder and harder.
Dad drives slower and slower.
It is getting later and later.

A policeman comes over.
"The road is closed,"
he tells my parents.
"There is too much water."

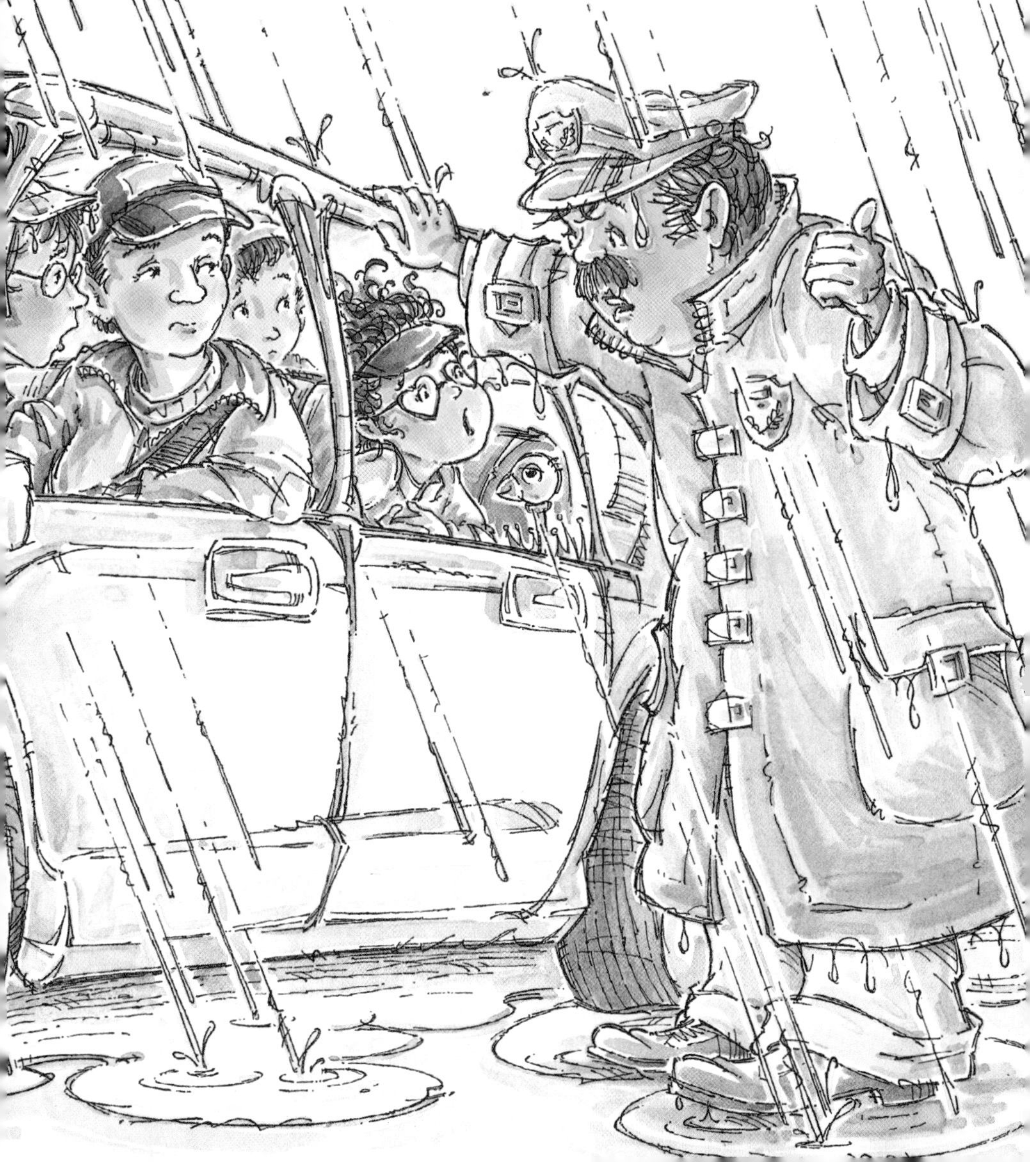

Oh no!

There are cars in front of us.

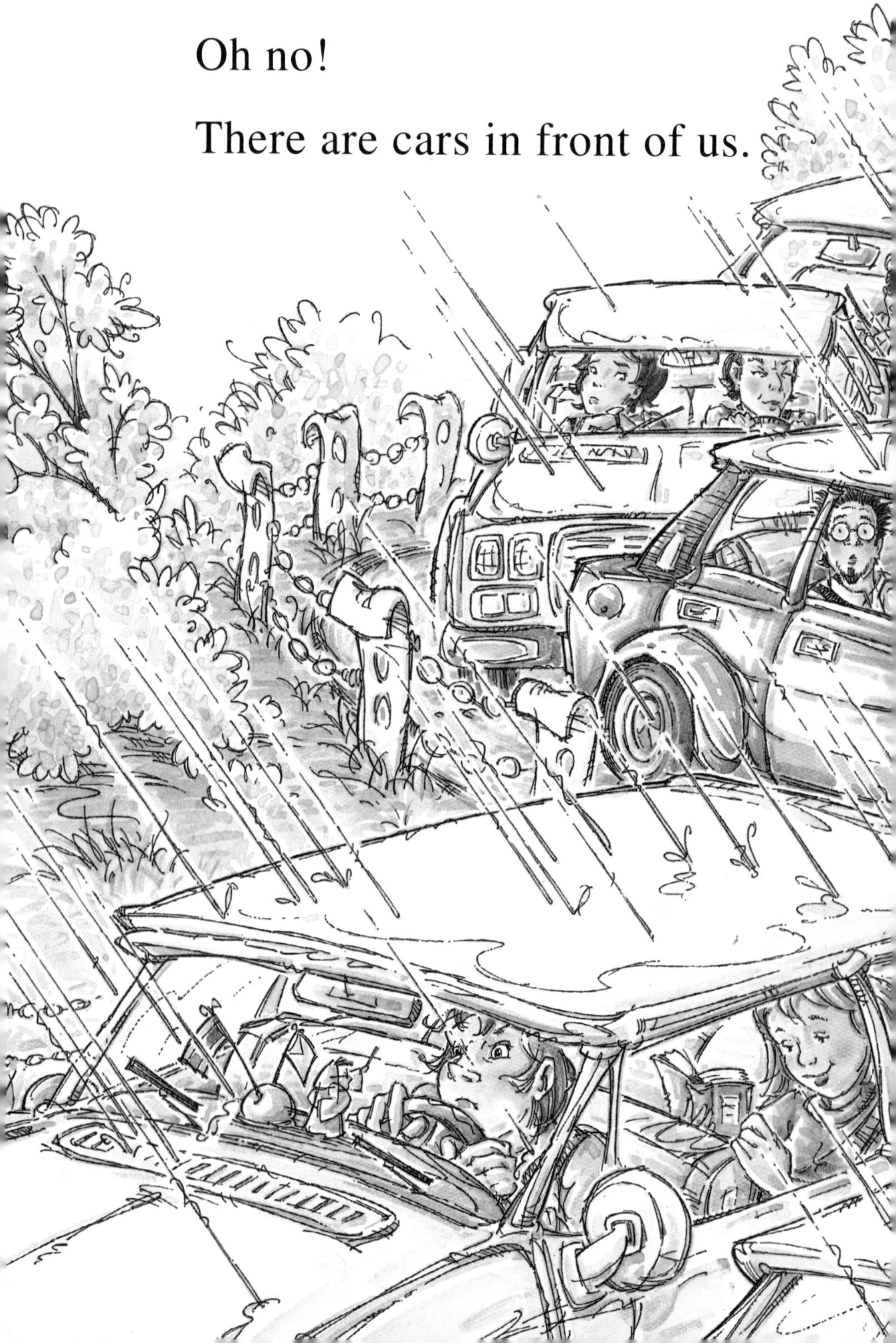

There are cars behind us.

We are stuck!

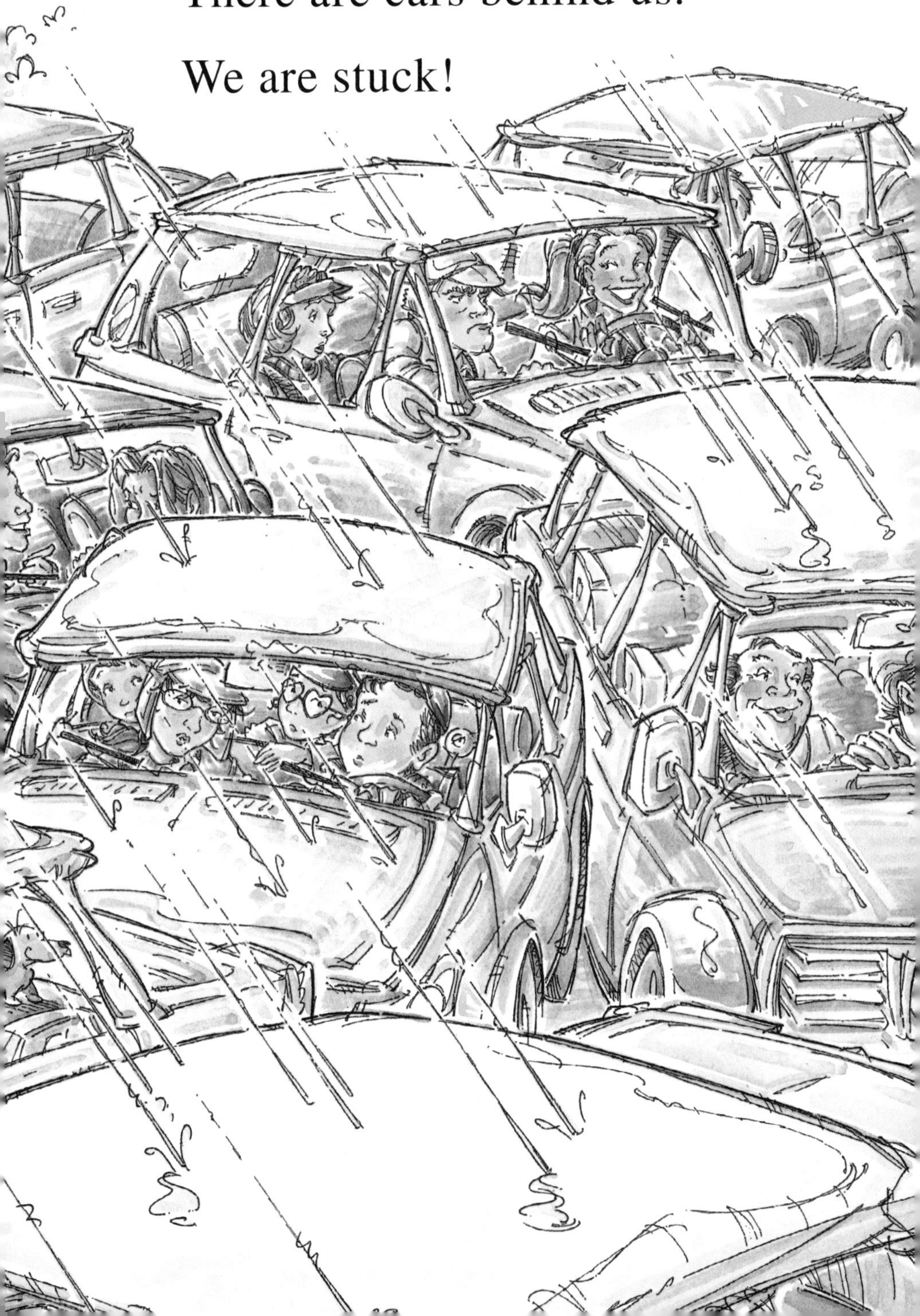

"The show is starting soon!"

Robert says.

"We will not make it."

Drip, drip, drip goes the rain.

Drip, drip, drip go my tears.

Robert and I are so sad.

We do not even want any cookies.

At last the cars move

and the rain stops.

But it is too late.

The night sky show is over.

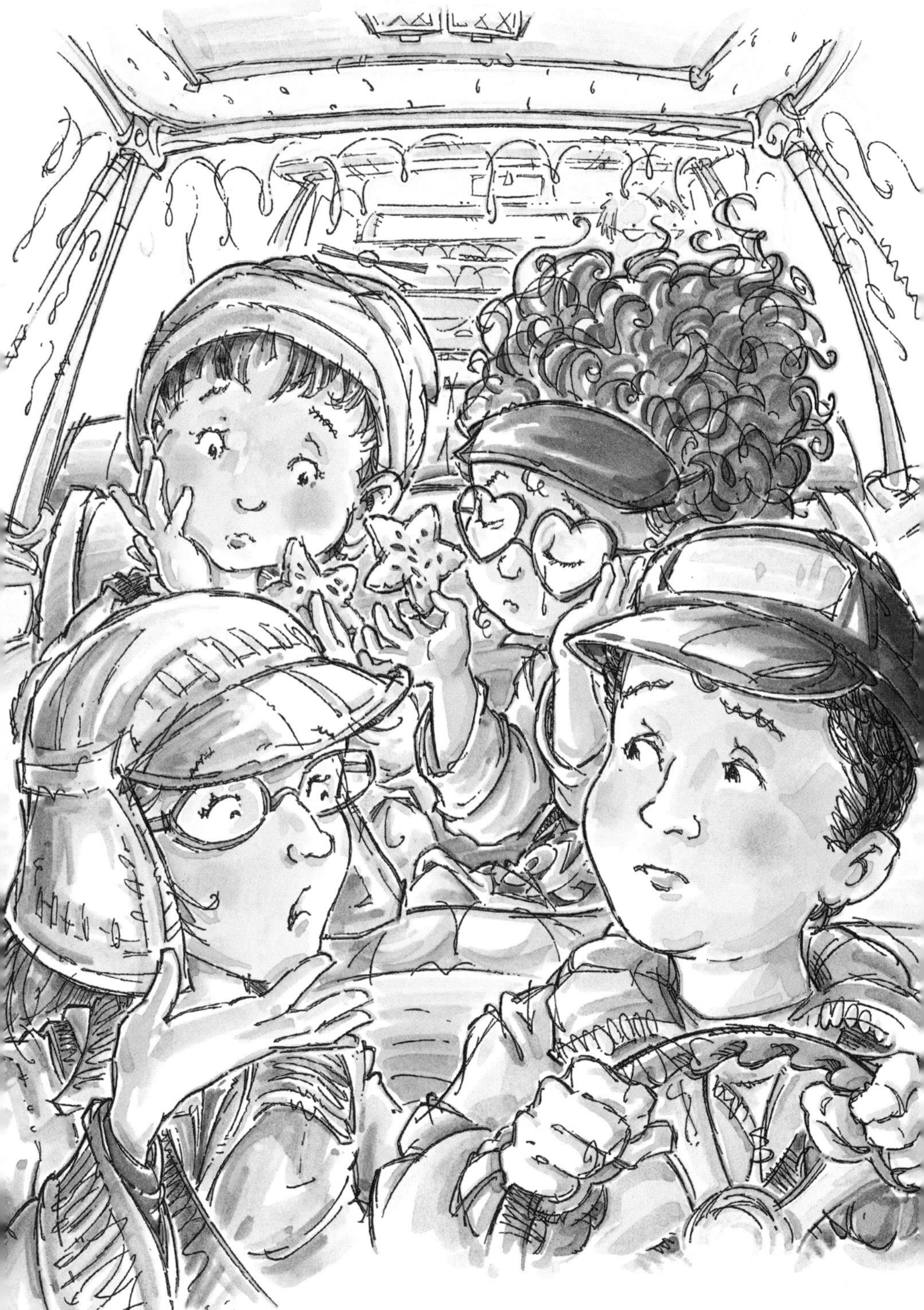

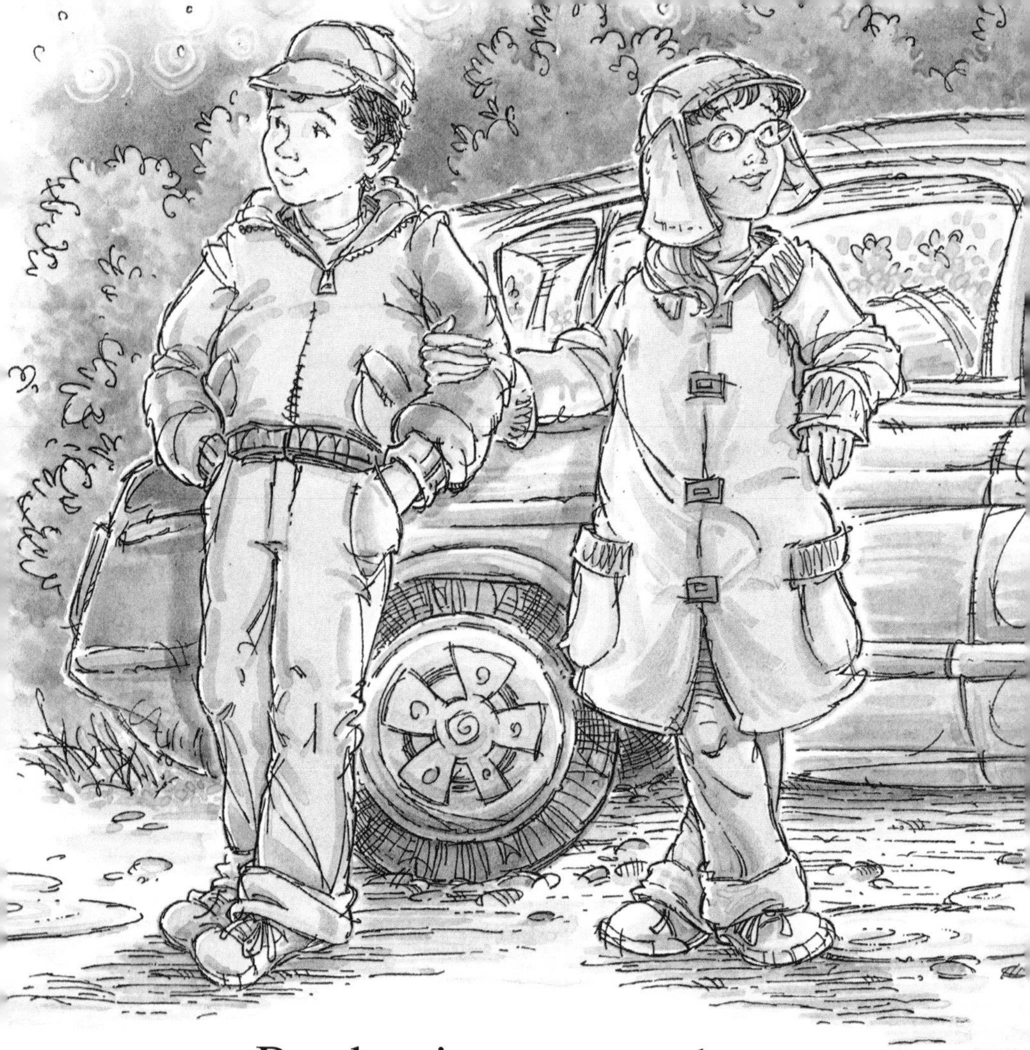

By the time we get home,
the sky is full of stars.
They are brilliant!
(That's a fancy word
for shiny and bright.)

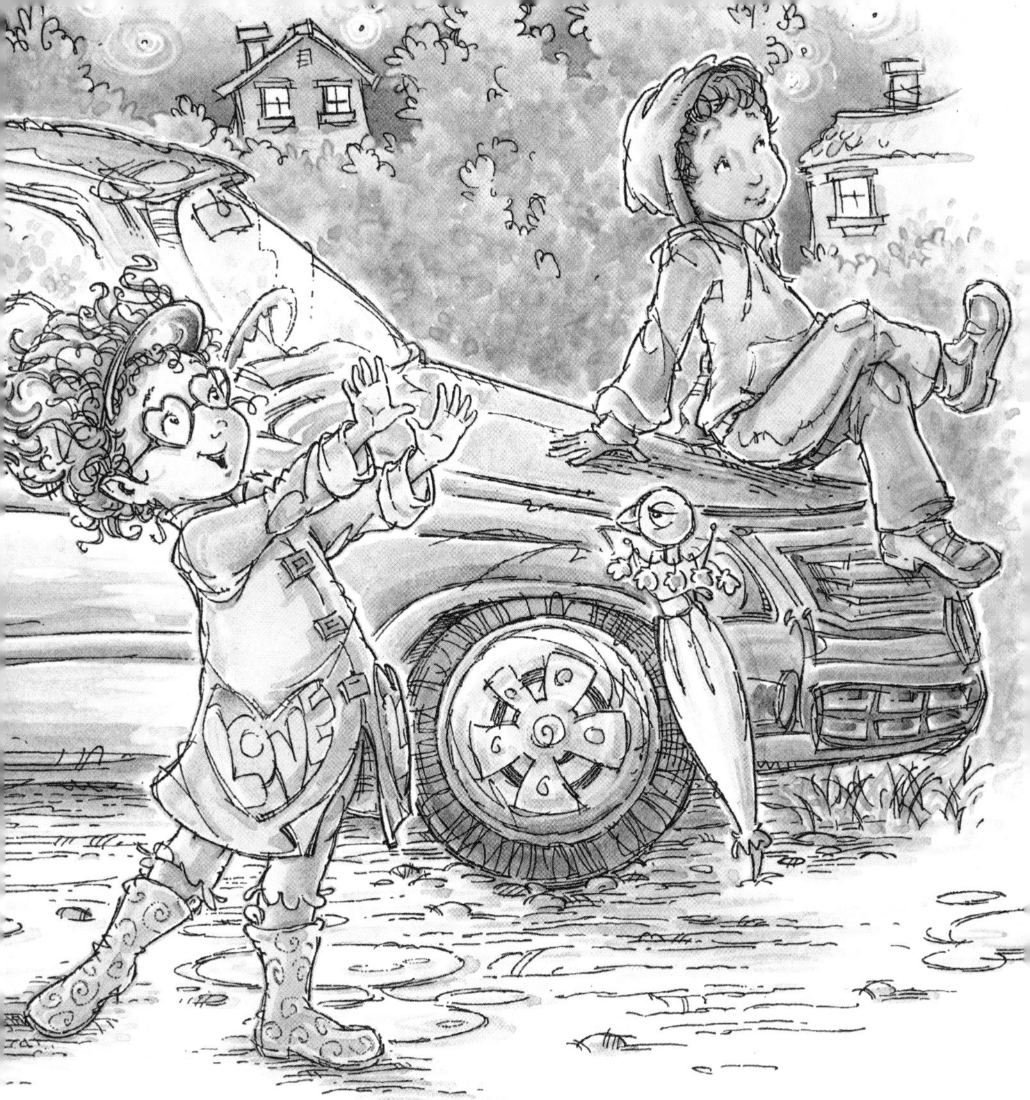
LOVE

I get a brilliant idea.

(Brilliant also means very smart.)

We can have

our own night sky show.

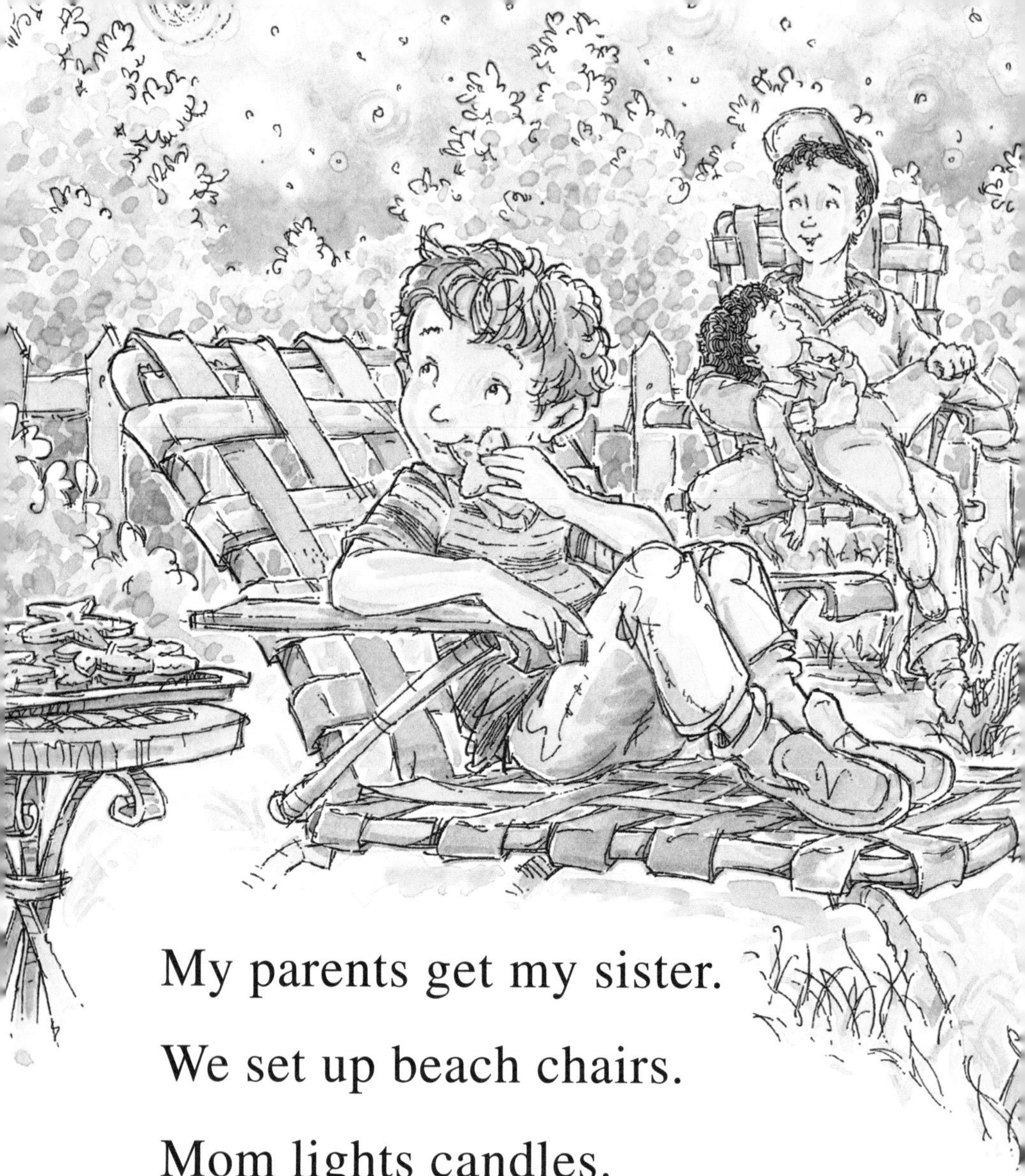

My parents get my sister.

We set up beach chairs.

Mom lights candles.

Dad puts the cookies on a tray.

We eat alfresco.

(That's fancy for eating outdoors.)

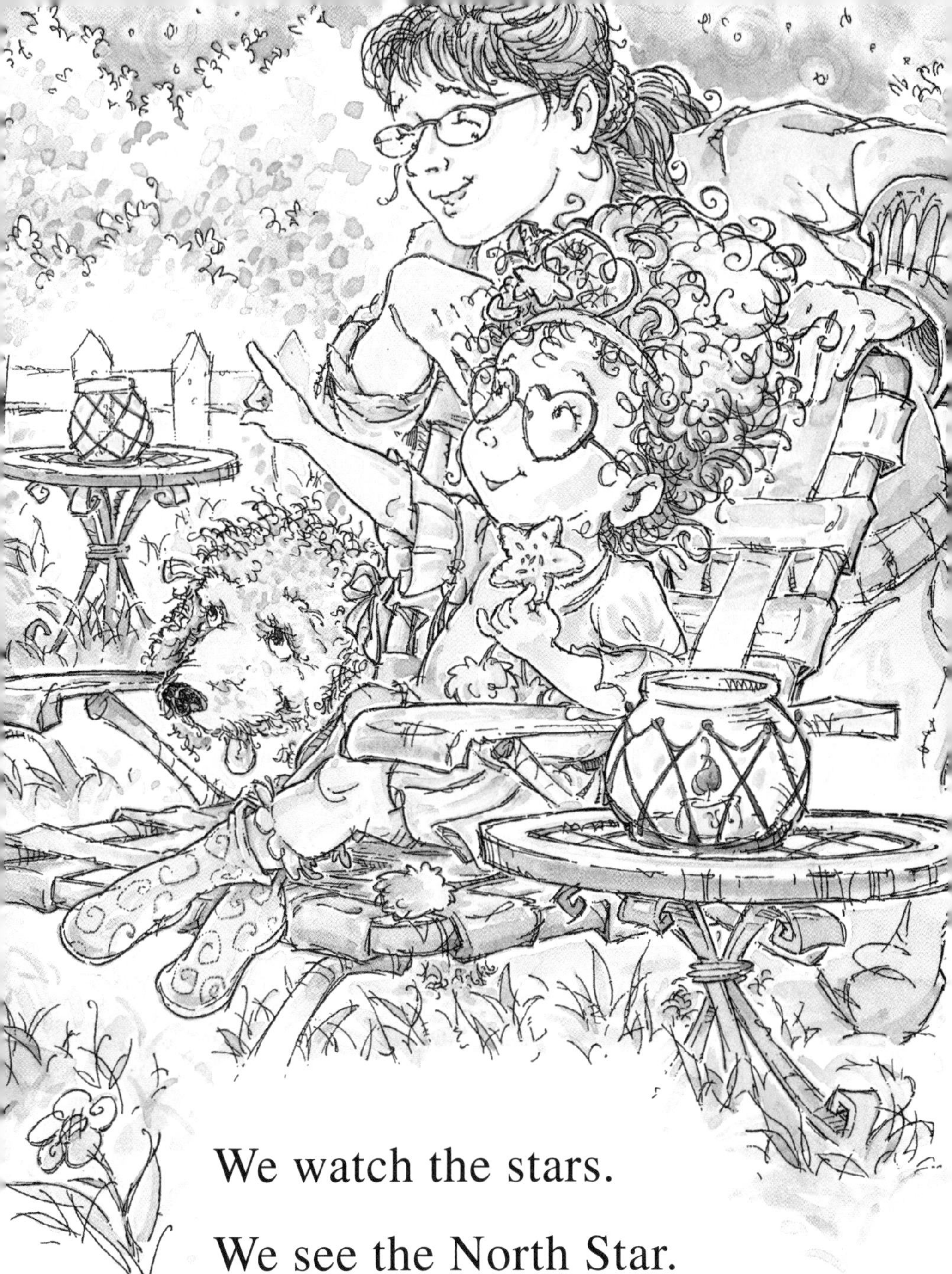

We watch the stars.

We see the North Star.

We see the Big Dipper.

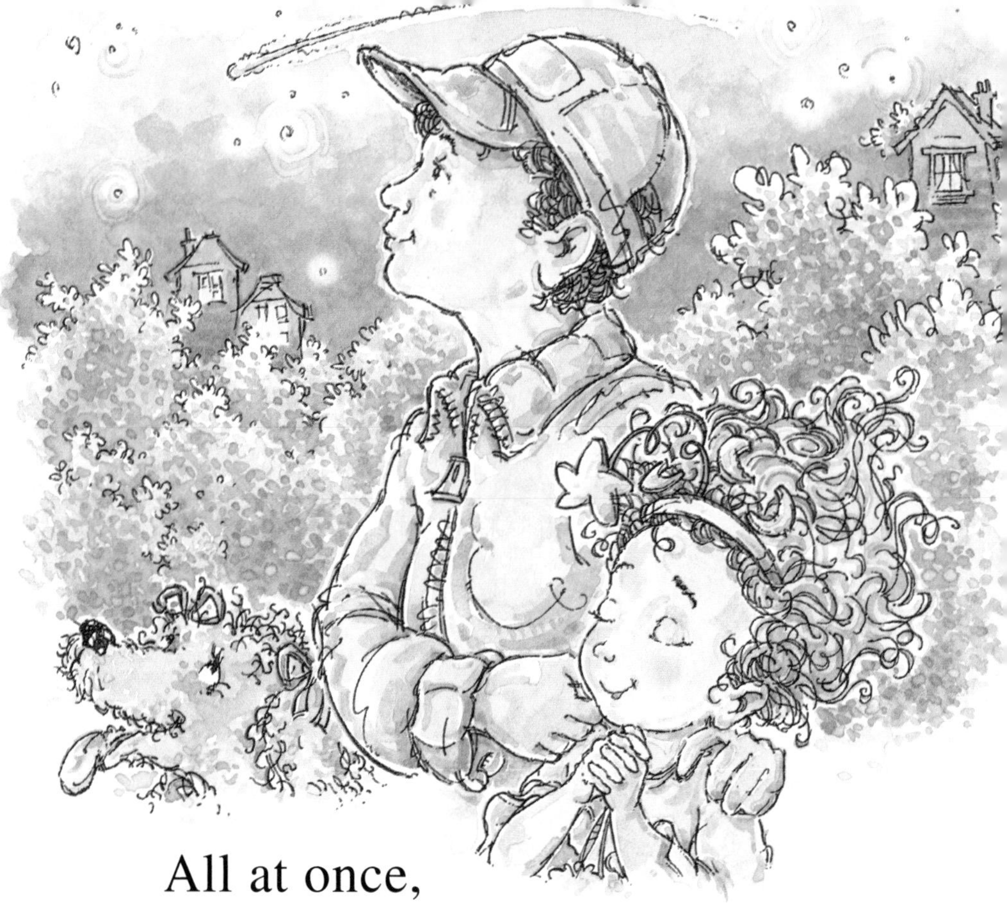

All at once,

something zooms across the sky.

“A shooting star,” Dad says.

“Make a wish!”

I tell Dad it is not a star.

It is a meteor.

But I make a wish anyway.

The next day Ms. Glass says,
"Everyone missed the show
because of the storm.
So we will go next week."
Everybody is very happy.
And guess what? My wish came true!

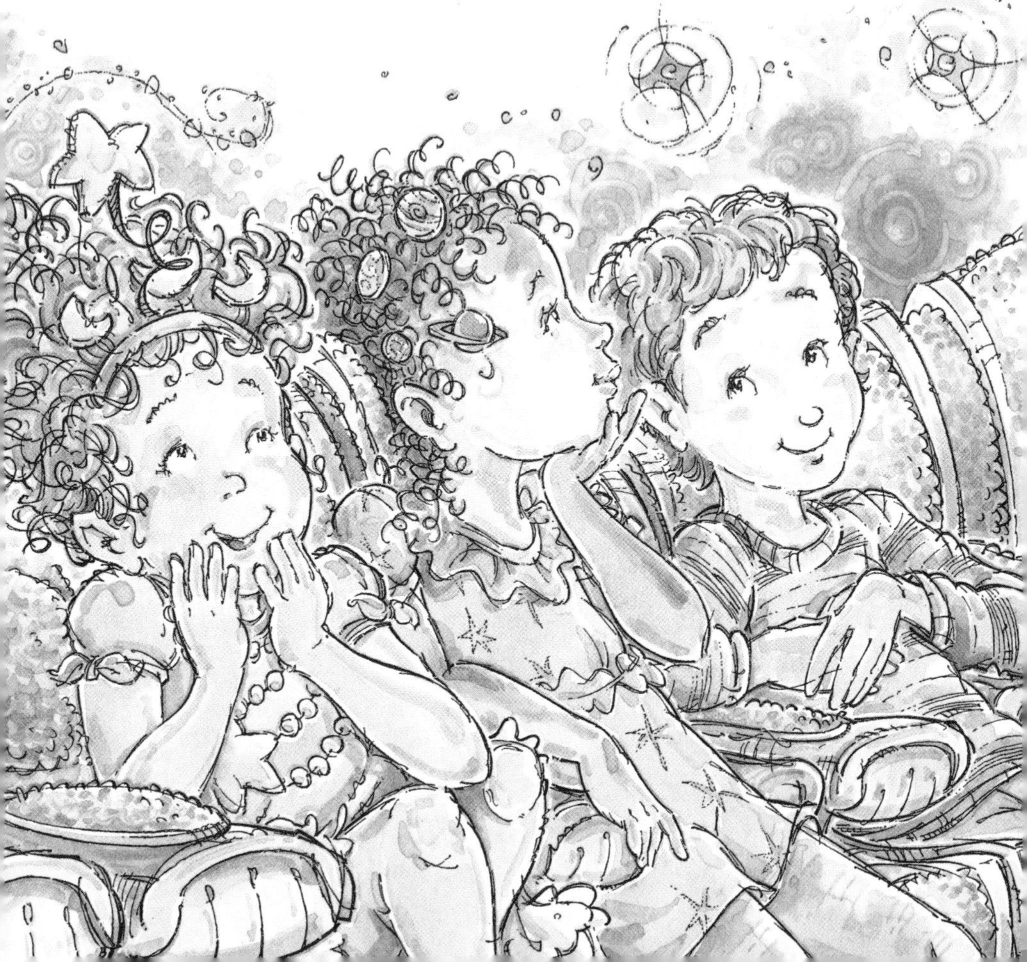

Fancy Nancy's Fancy Words

These are the fancy words in this book:

Alfresco—outside; eating outside is called eating alfresco

Brilliant—bright and shiny, or very, very smart

Constellation—a group of stars that make a picture

Fascinating—very interesting

Meteor—a piece of a comet that leaves a blazing streak as it travels across the sky (you say it like this: me-tee-or)

Orbit—to circle around something

Planetarium—a museum about stars and planets

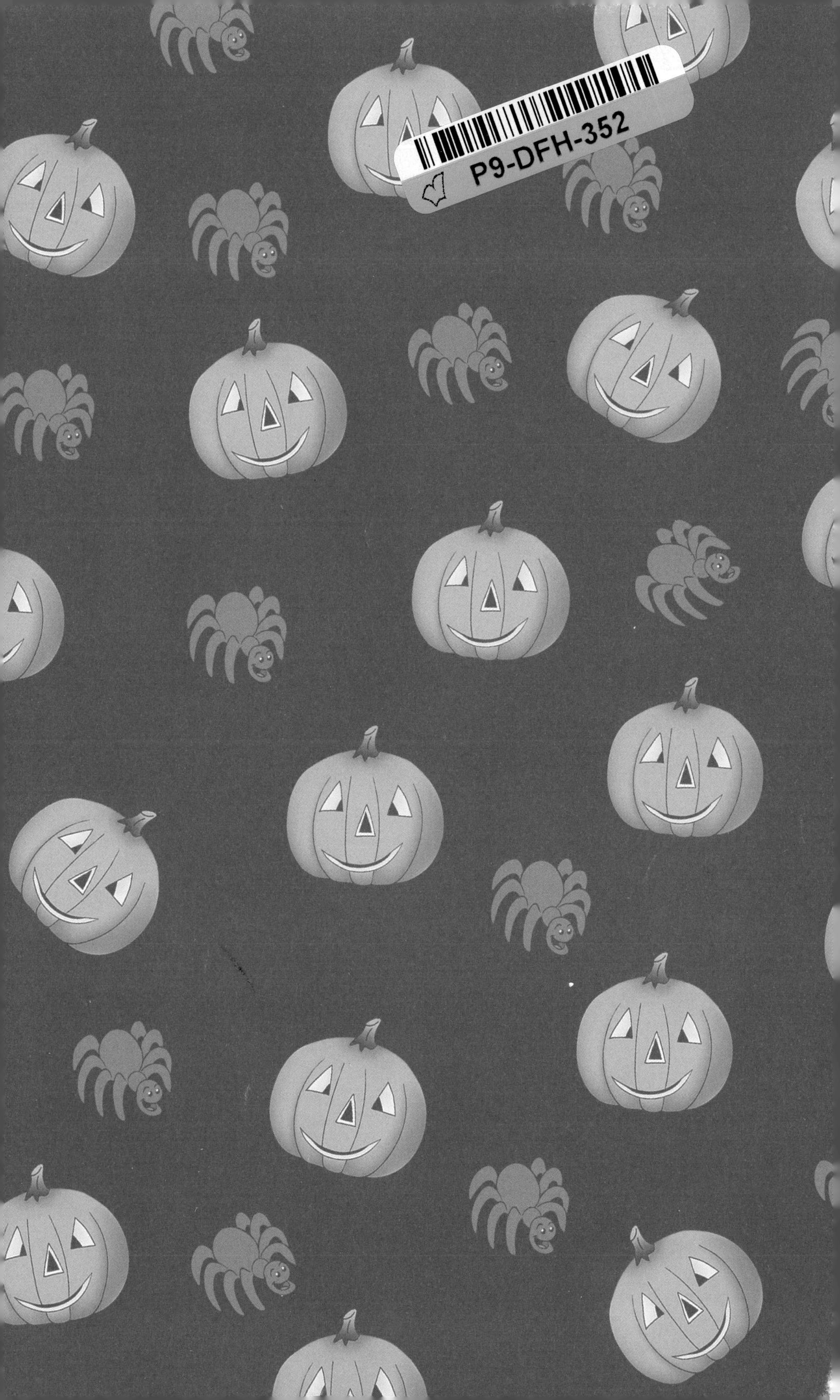

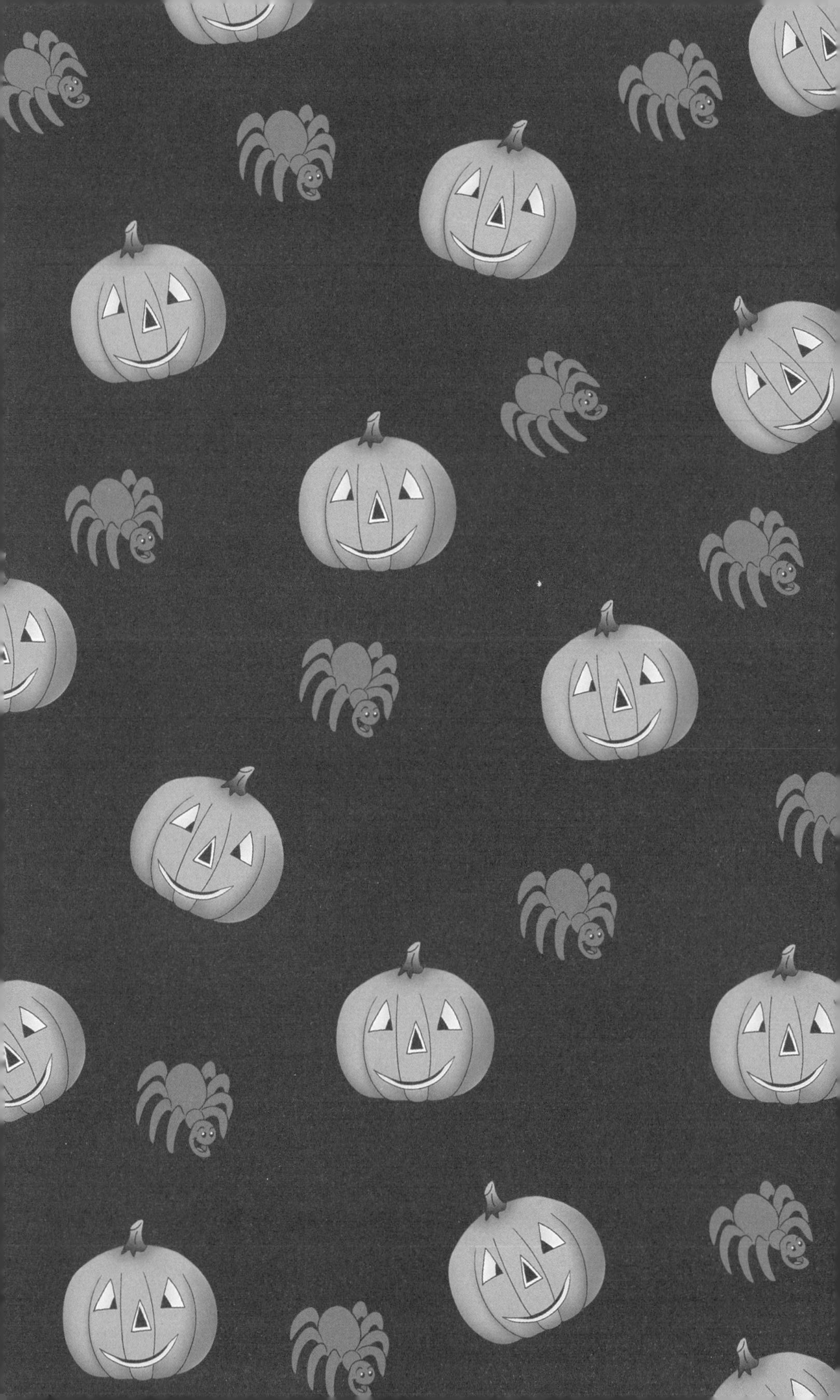

Curious George®
Haunted Halloween

Adaptation by C. A. Krones
Based on the TV special
Curious George: A Halloween Boo Fest
written by Joe Fallon

Houghton Mifflin Harcourt
Boston   New York

For information about permission to reproduce selections from this book, write to Permissions, Houghton Mifflin Harcourt Publishing Company, 215 Park Avenue South, New York, New York 10003.

ISBN: 978-0-544-32077-2 paper-over-board
ISBN: 978-0-544-32079-6 paperback

Design by Afsoon Razavi

www.hmhco.com

Printed in China
SCP 10 9 8 7 6 5 4 3 2 1
4500466719

AGES	GRADES	GUIDED READING LEVEL	READING RECOVERY LEVEL	LEXILE ® LE
5–7	1	J	17	480L

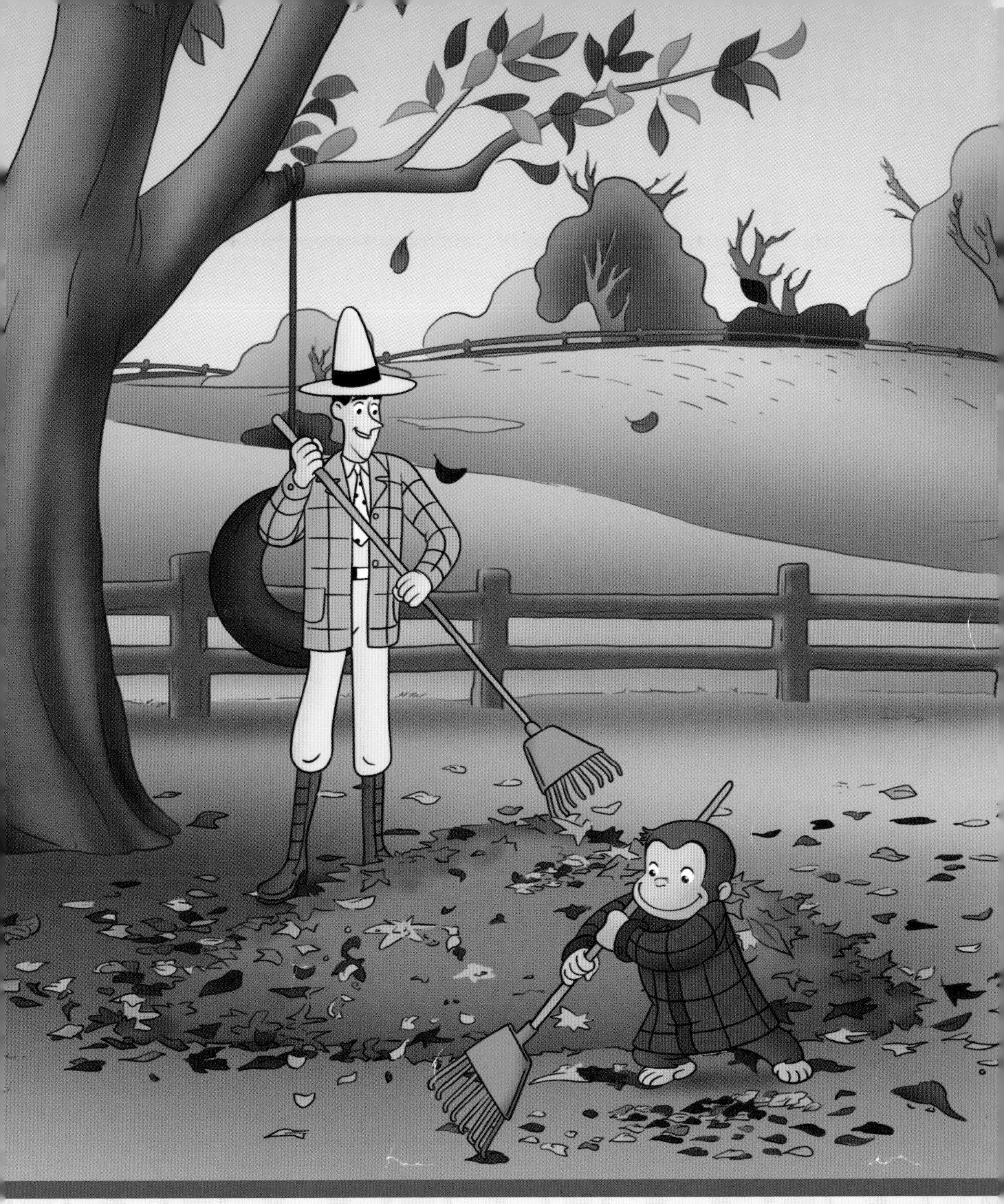

This year, George was spending
Halloween in the country.
The last autumn leaves were falling.
George and the man with the yellow
hat were busy raking.

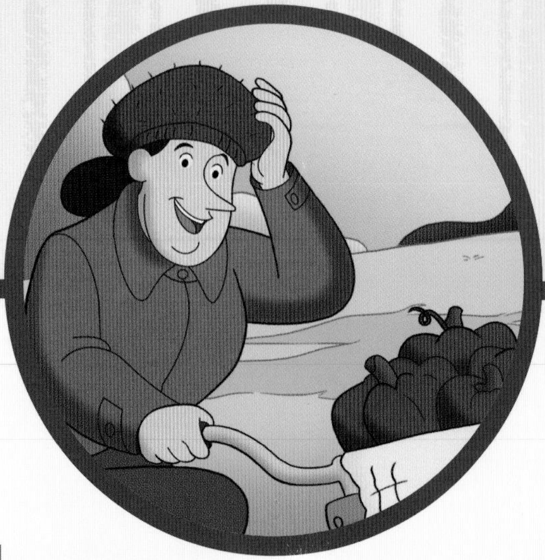

Mrs. Renkins rode
by on her bicycle.
"Halloween's here! Hang on to your hats!" she shouted.
"Happy Halloween, Mrs. Renkins!" said the man.
George was curious. Why would he need to hang on to his hat?

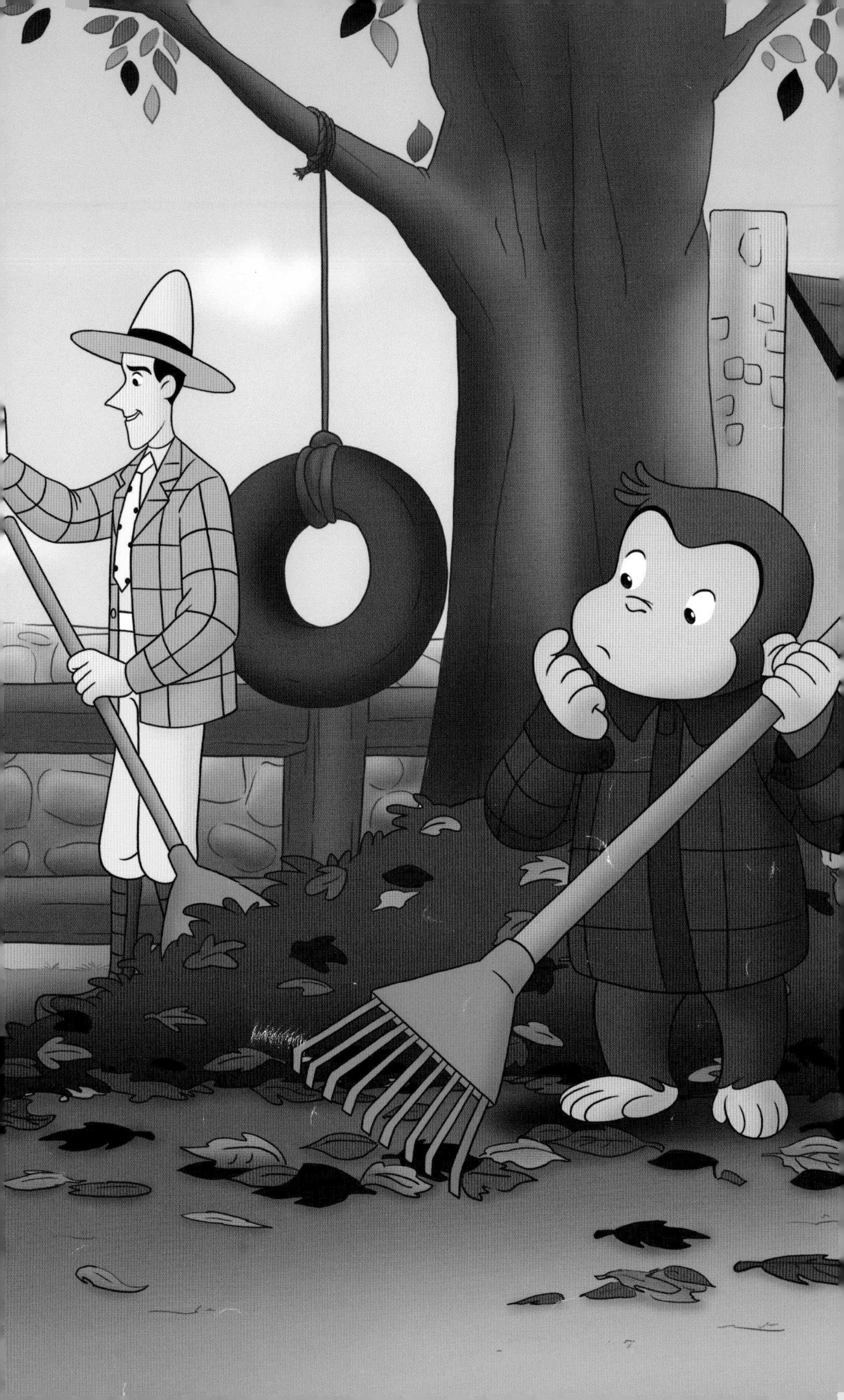

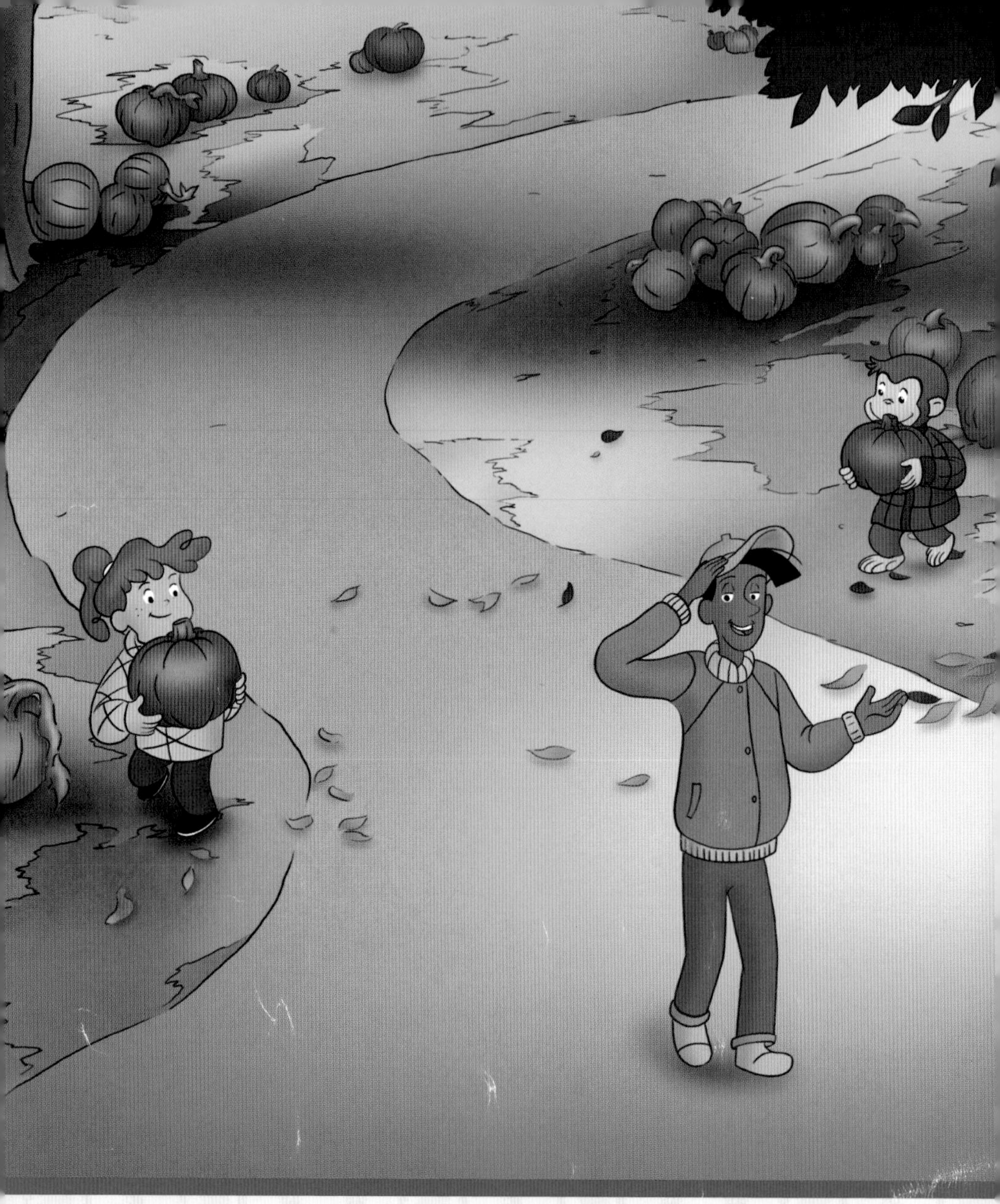

George went to the Renkinses' farm.
There were so many pumpkins!
His friends Allie and Bill were there, too.
"Hang on to your hats!" said Bill.

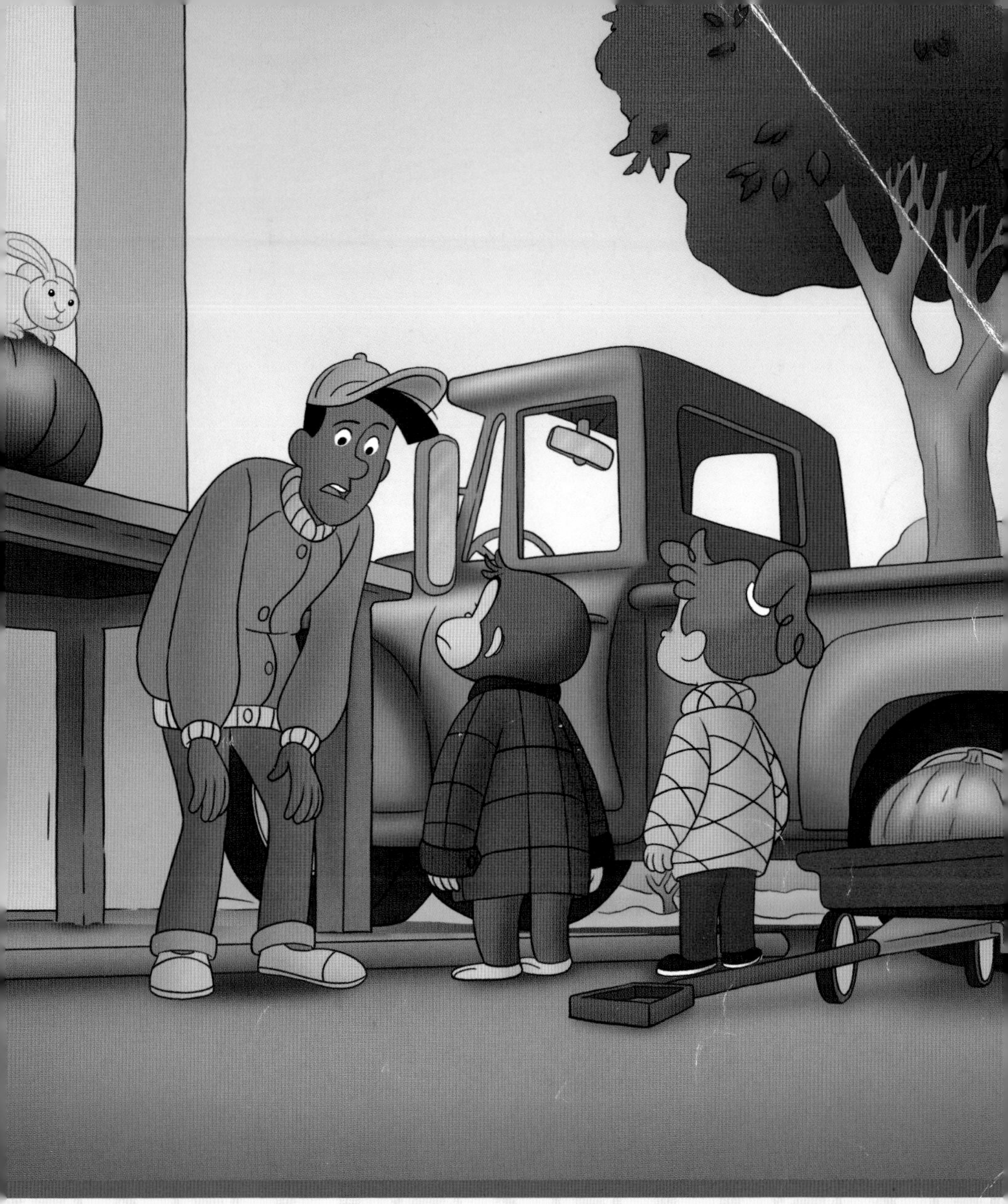

George and Allie were confused.
Why was everyone saying that?
"Haven't you heard of the Legend of
No Noggin?" Bill asked.
They hadn't.

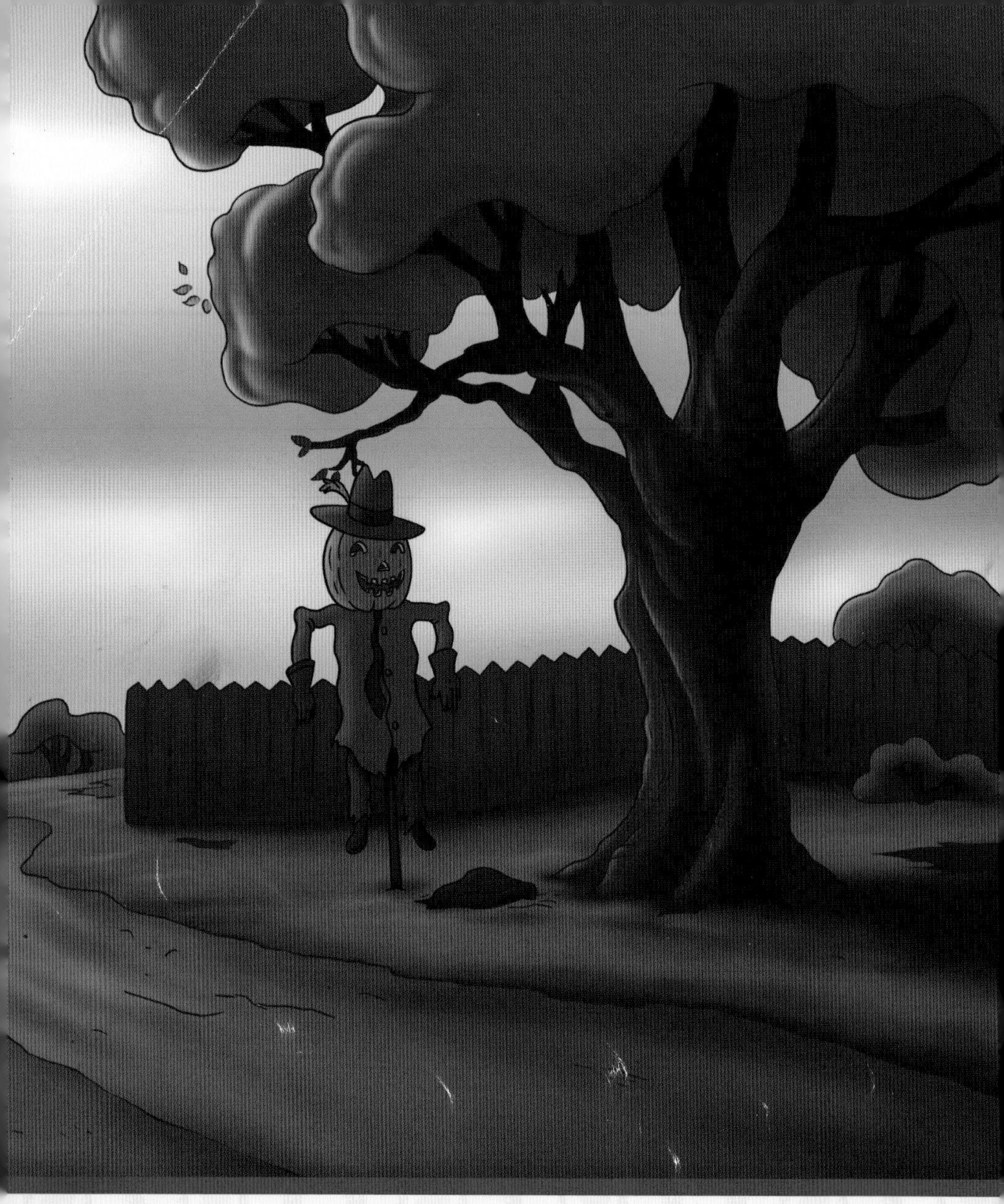

Then Bill told them the spooky story:
A long time ago, there was a scarecrow perched by Old Lonesome Tree.
It had a big pumpkin for a head, and a hat on top.

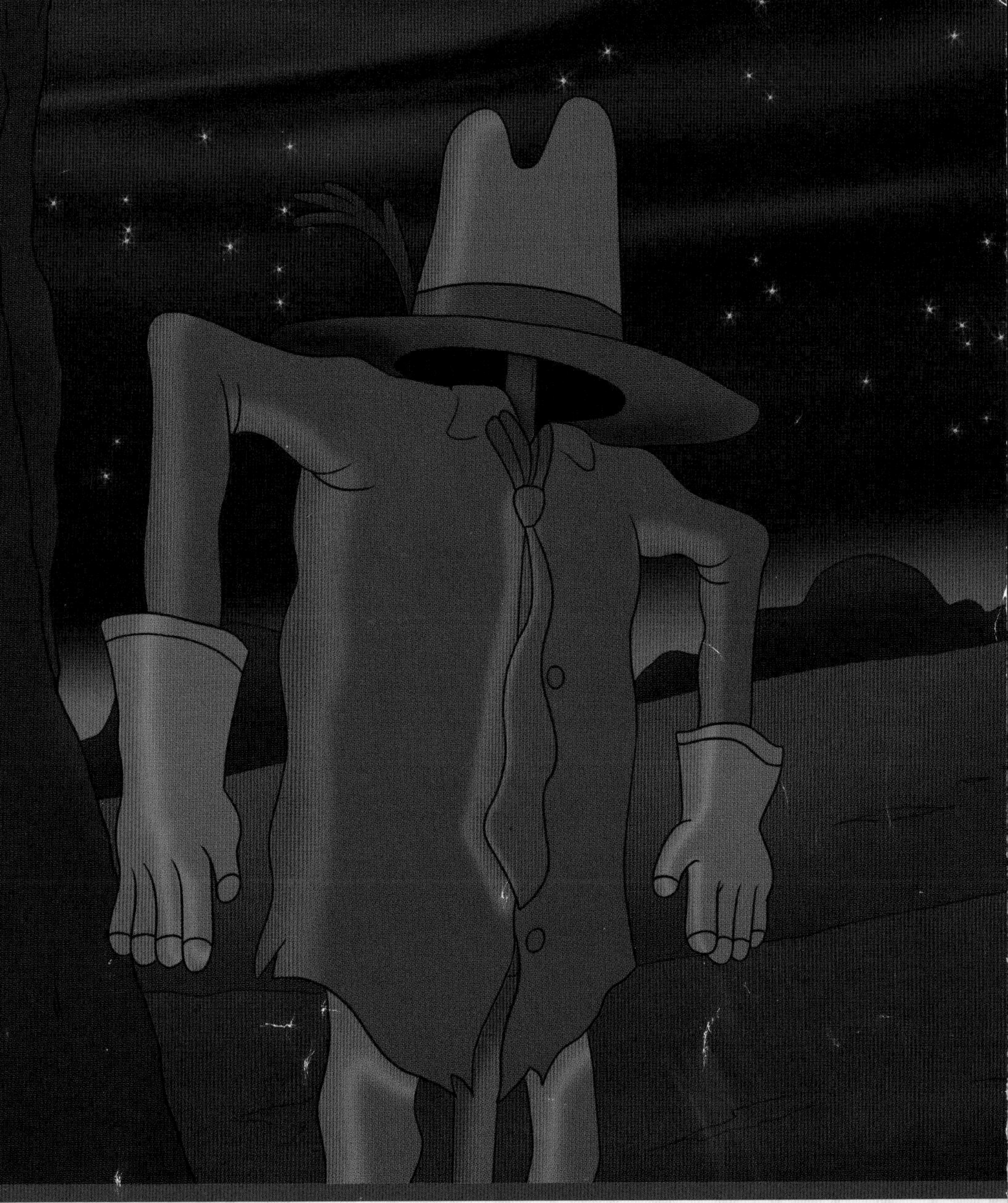

But one Halloween, the pumpkin went missing.
From then on, everybody called the scarecrow No Noggin because it had no head.

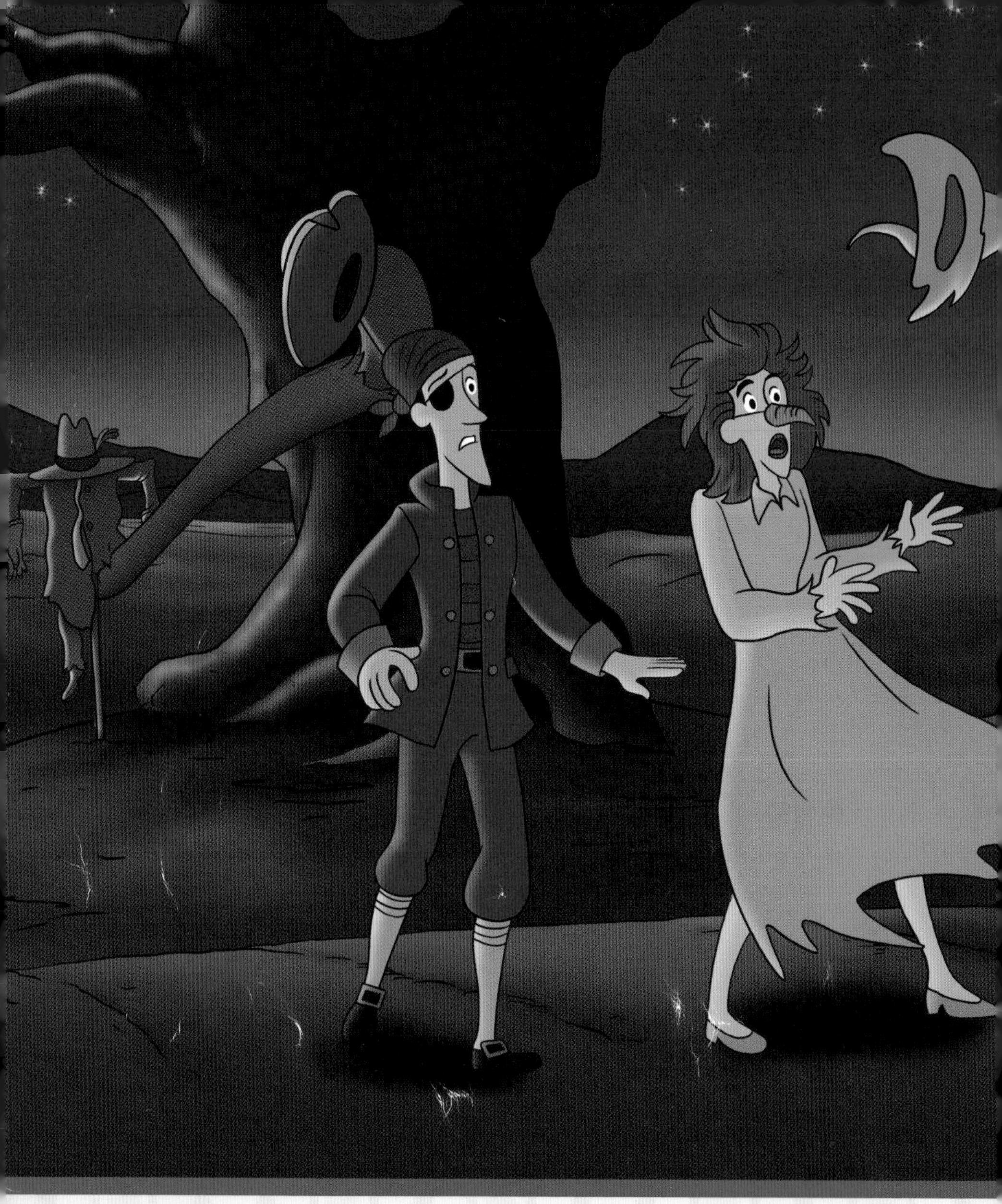

No Noggin was angry.
What good was a hat without a head?
That's why every Halloween night, No Noggin shows up and kicks people's hats off!

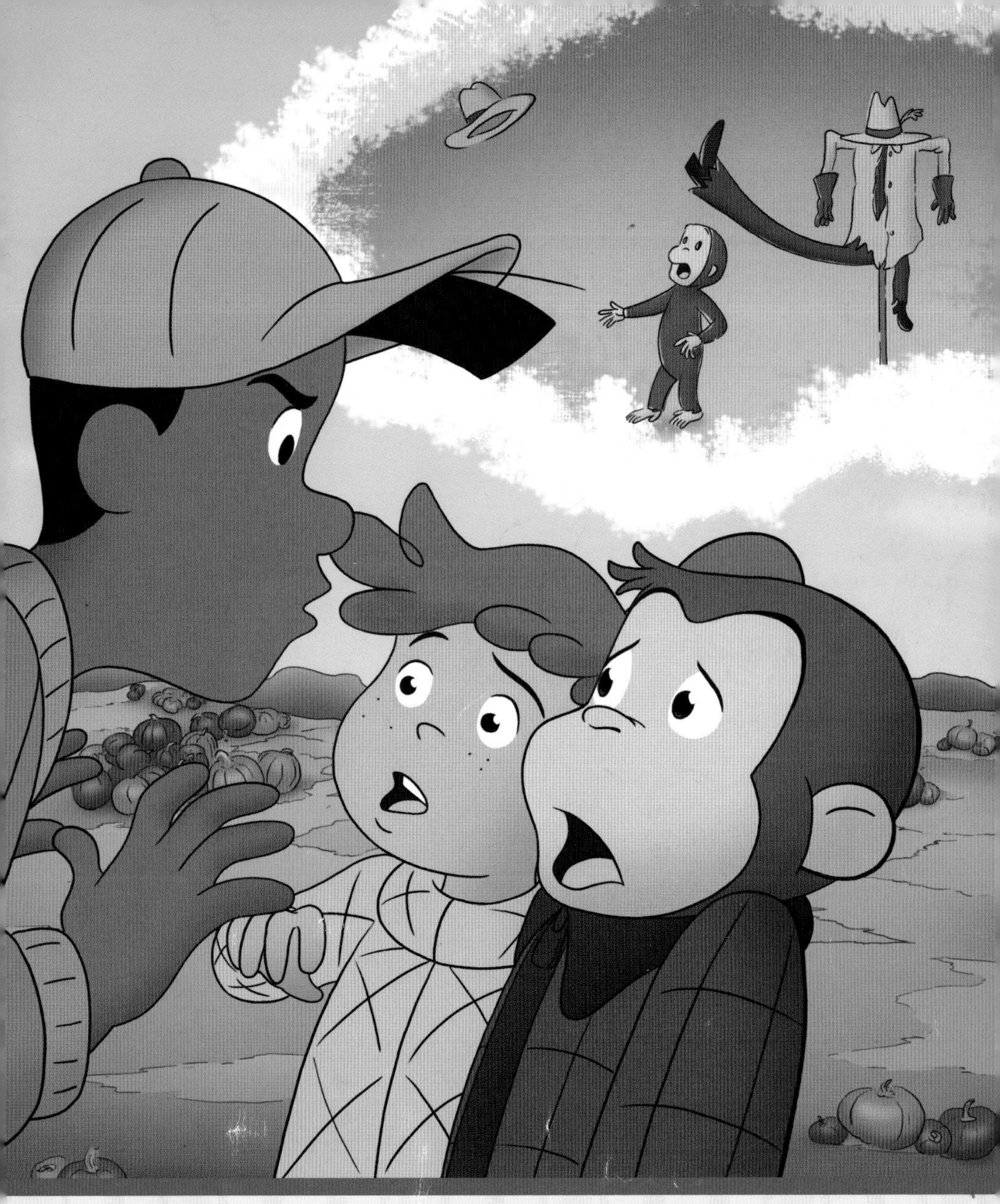

George was spooked!
A headless scarecrow ghost?
"Don't worry," said Bill. "Just make sure you hang on to your hat on Halloween."

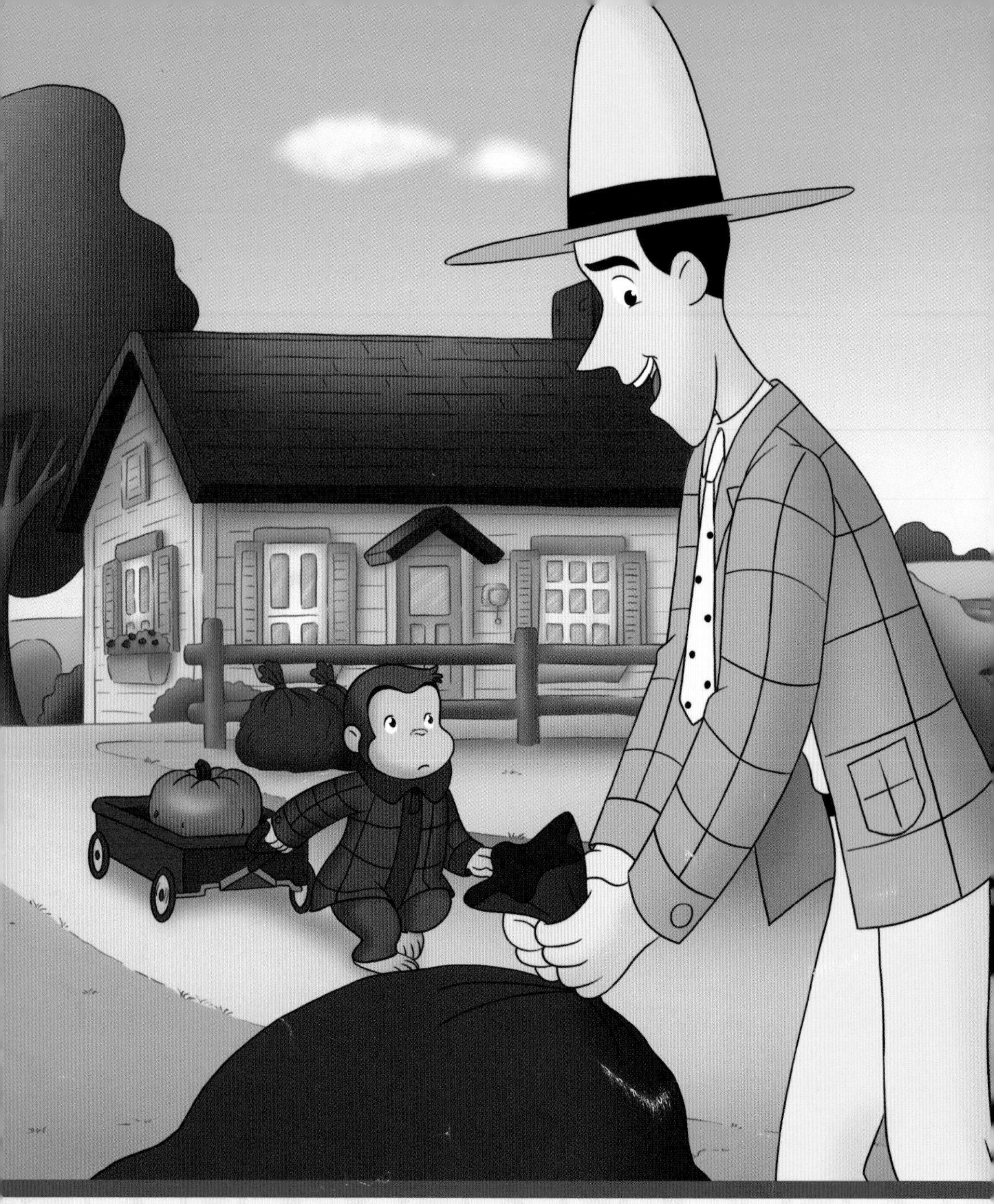

George went home with his pumpkin.
He wanted to see his friend and find
out more about No Noggin.

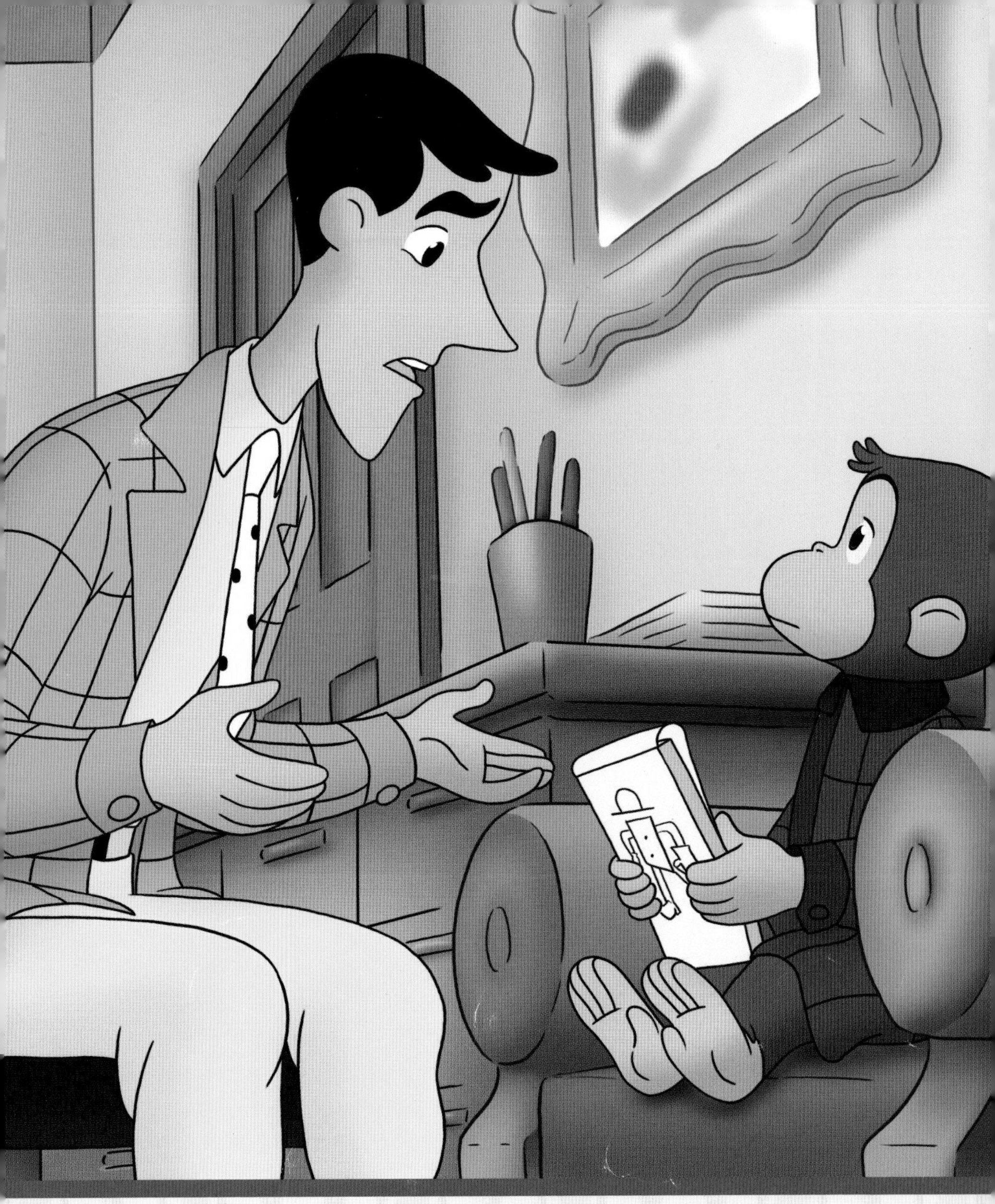

“It’s just a legend, George,” said the man, “a tall tale, a ghost story–it’s not real.”
But George wasn’t so sure.

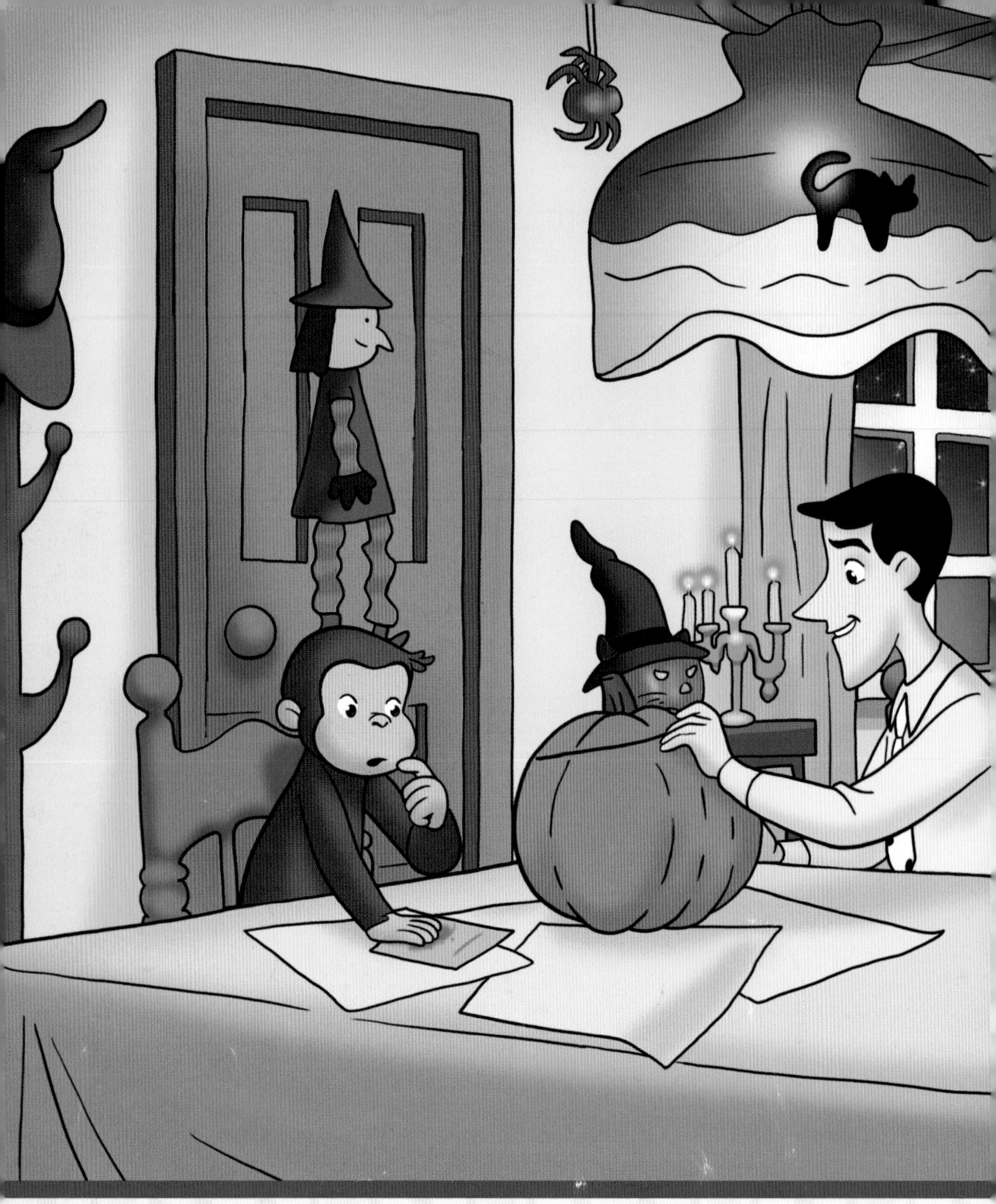

George and his friend decided to carve a jack-o'-lantern.
George tried to get his mind off ghosts.
But he needed to know if No Noggin was real.

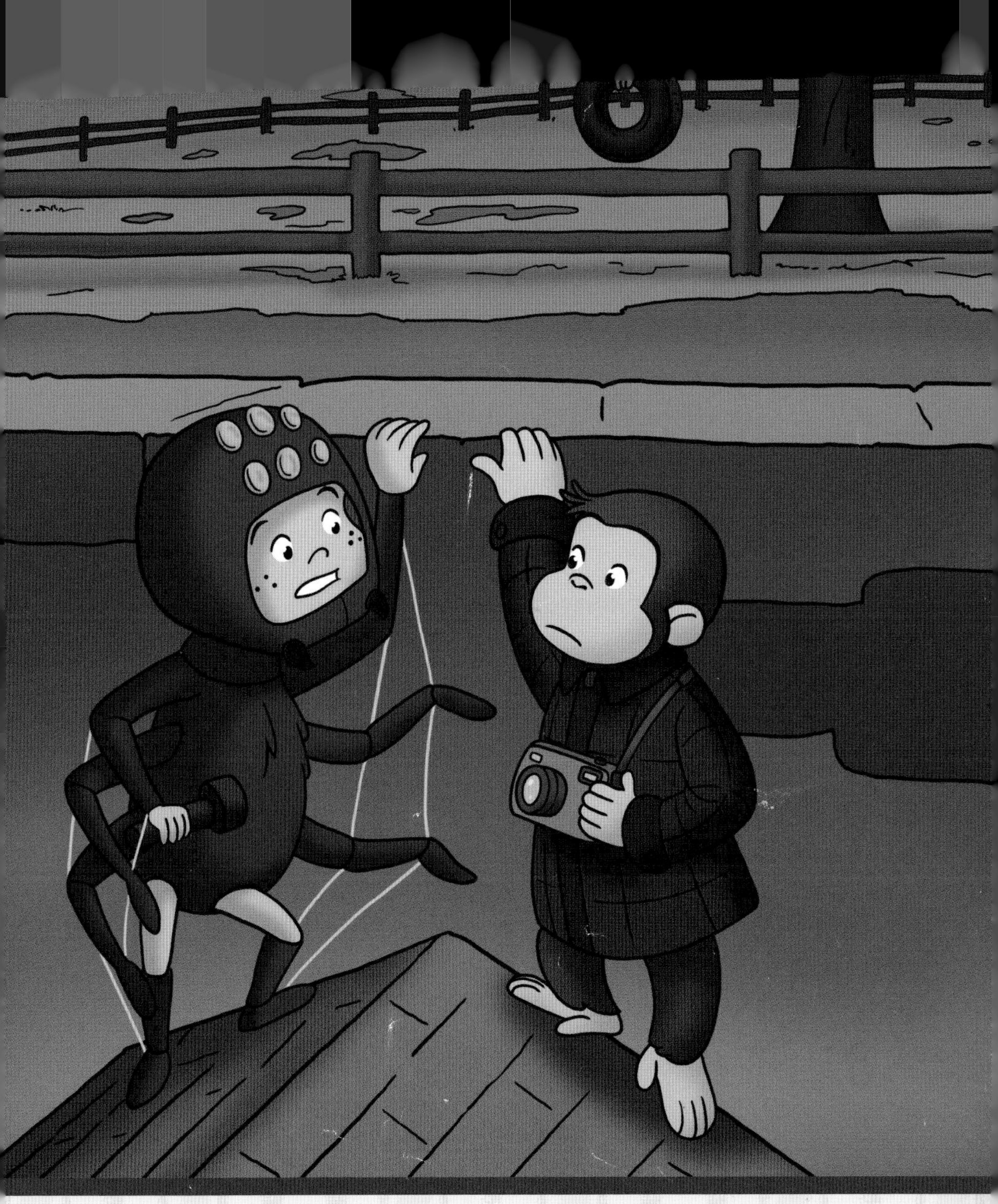

The next night was Halloween.
George and Allie were hiding near
Old Lonesome Tree.
They were going to catch No Noggin
on camera.

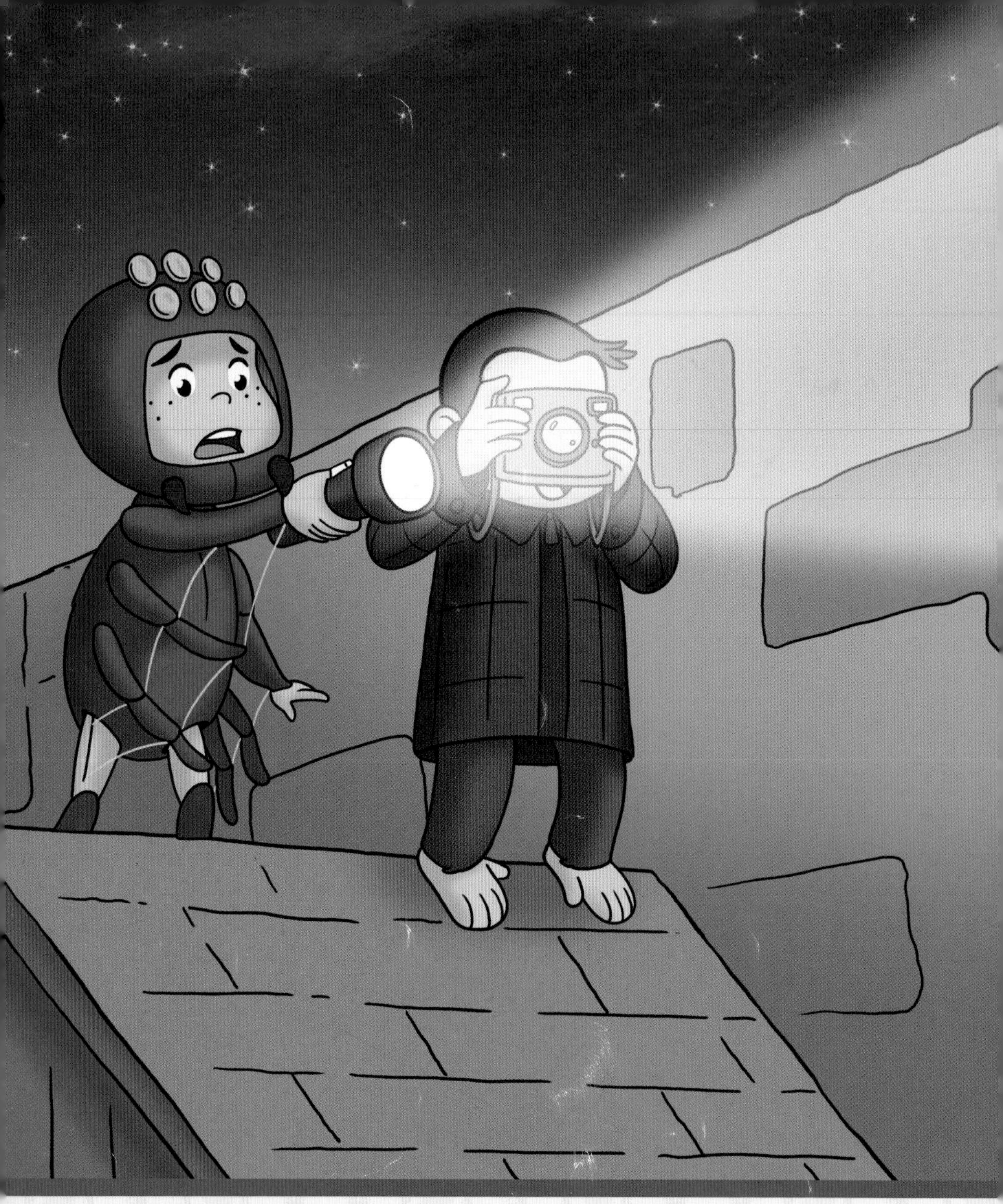

Suddenly, they saw a shadow!
Could it be No Noggin?
George took a photo.

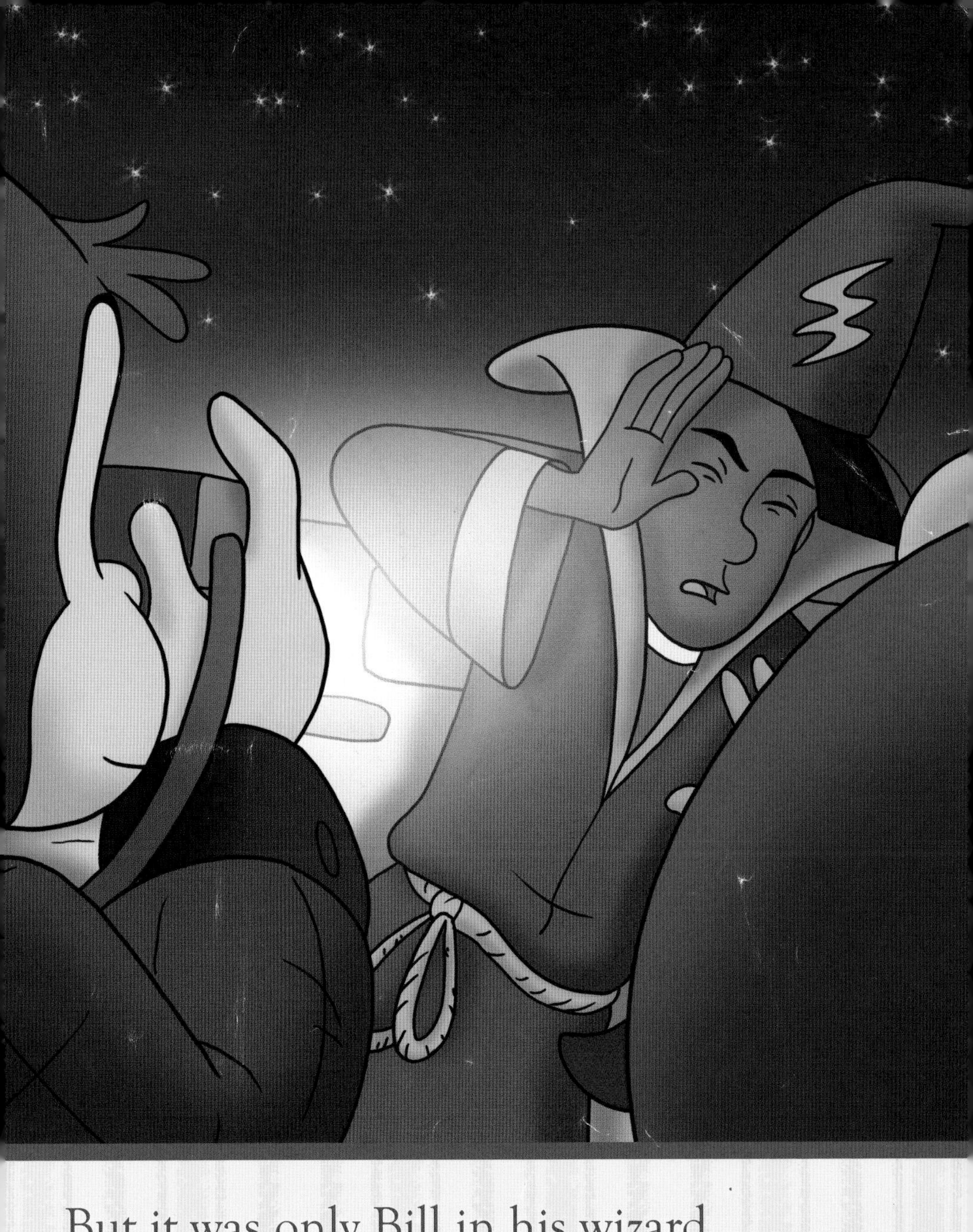

But it was only Bill in his wizard
costume.
Then George and Allie had an idea.
Bill could help catch No Noggin with
his wizard hat.

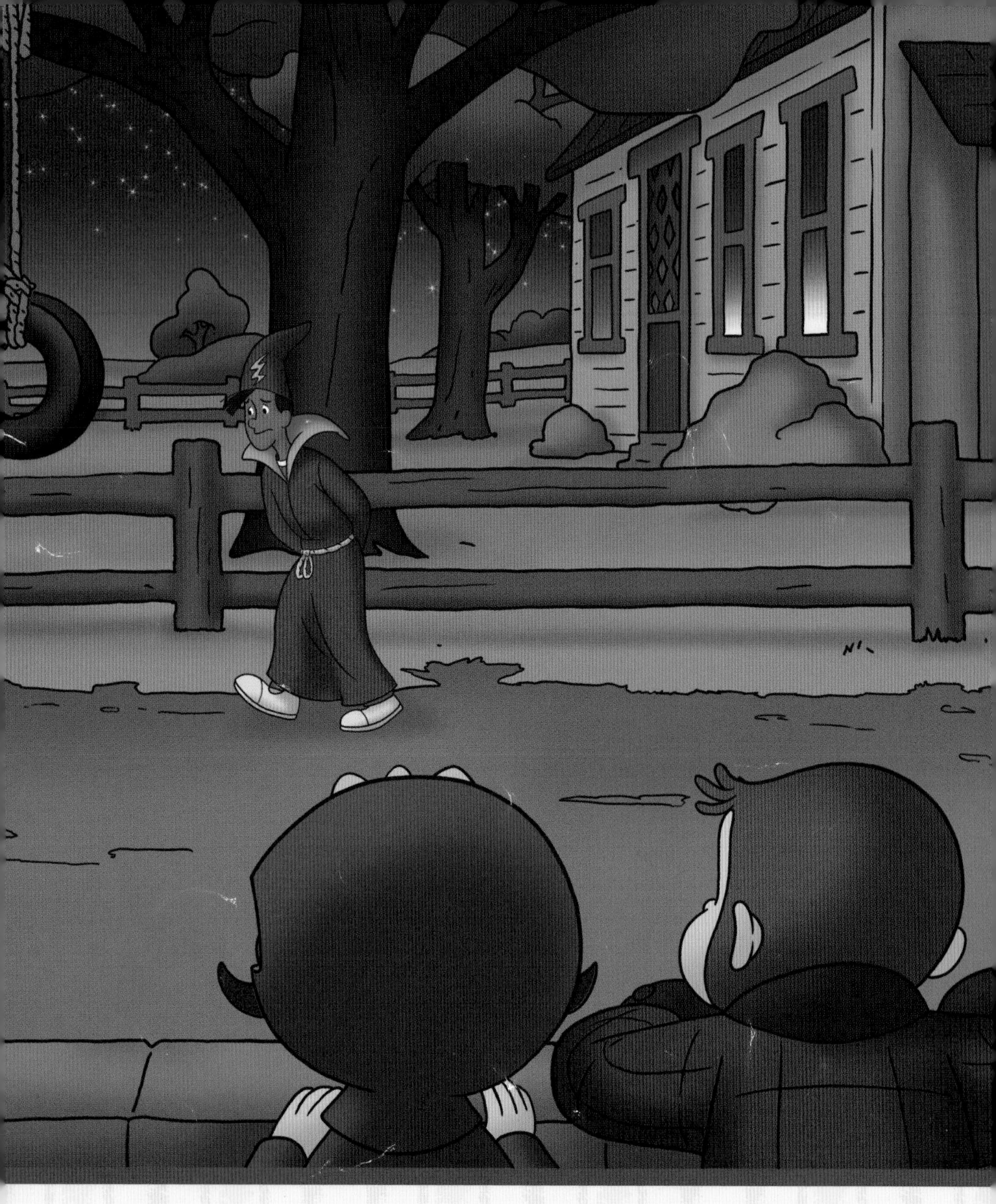

Bill stood near Old Lonesome Tree. He walked back and forth and waited for No Noggin to kick his hat.

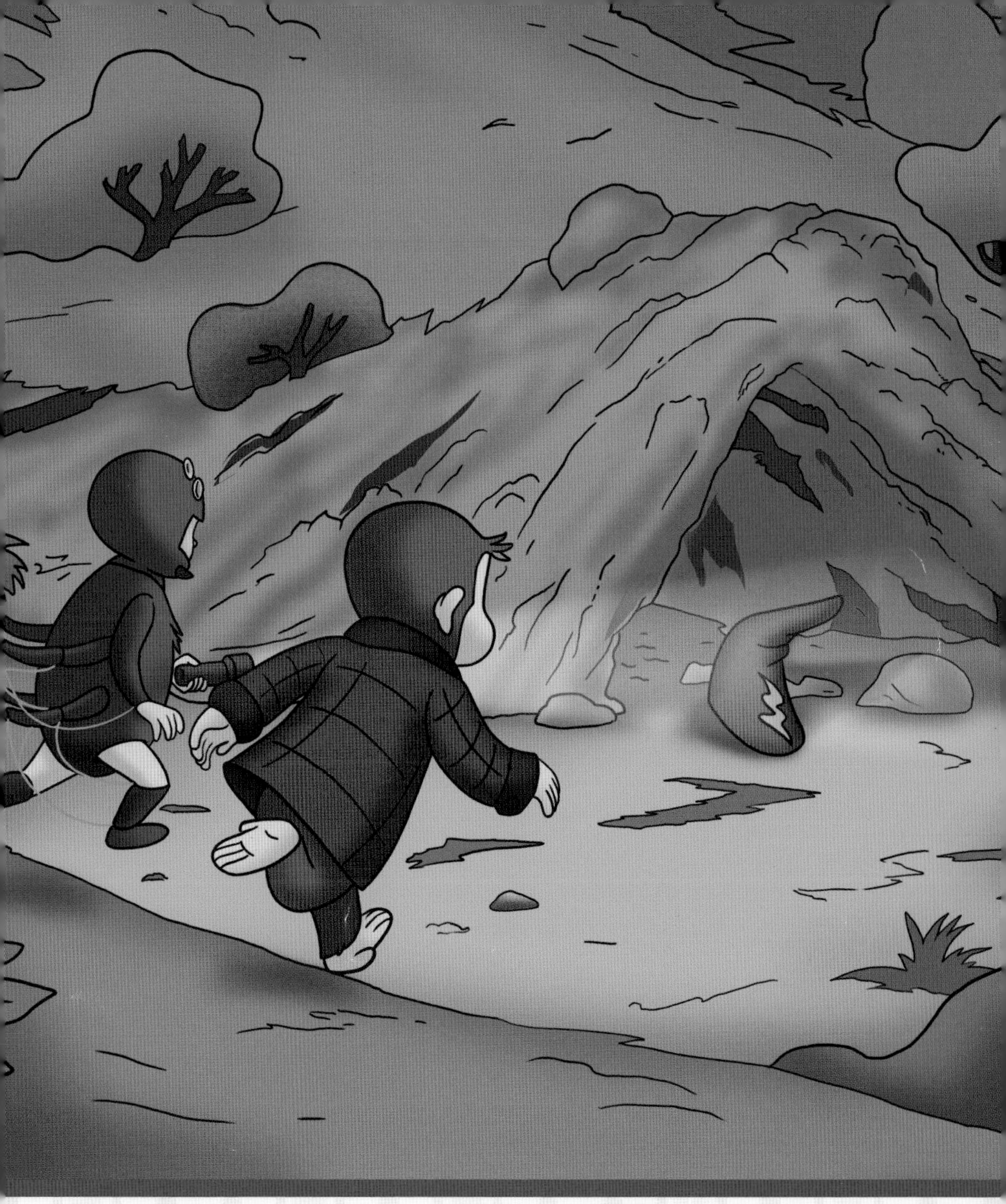

Suddenly, Bill's hat flew off his head! George and Allie chased the moving hat into a cave.

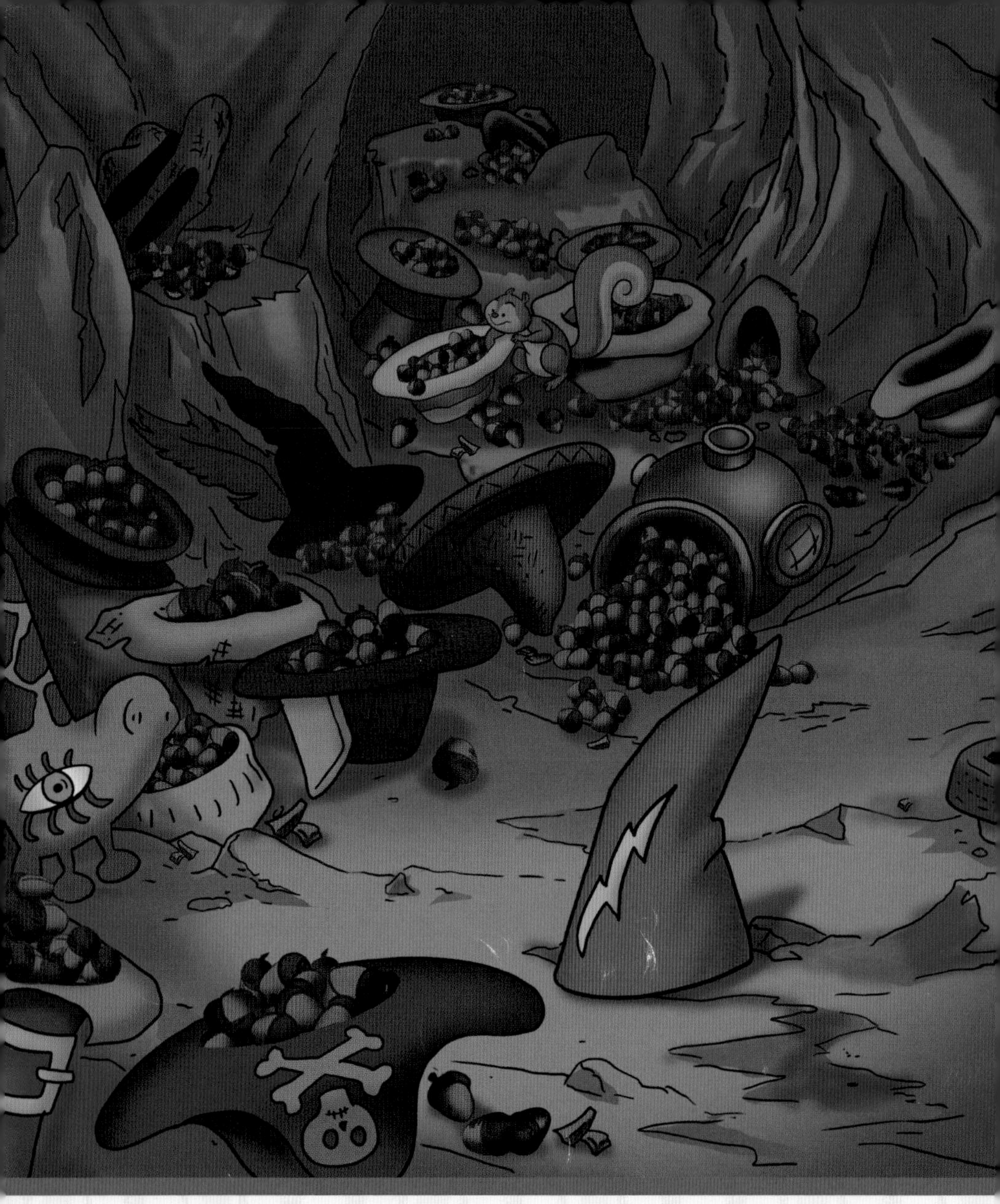

Inside the cave, they found Bill's hat.
And Jumpy Squirrel.
And lots of other hats, all filled with acorns!

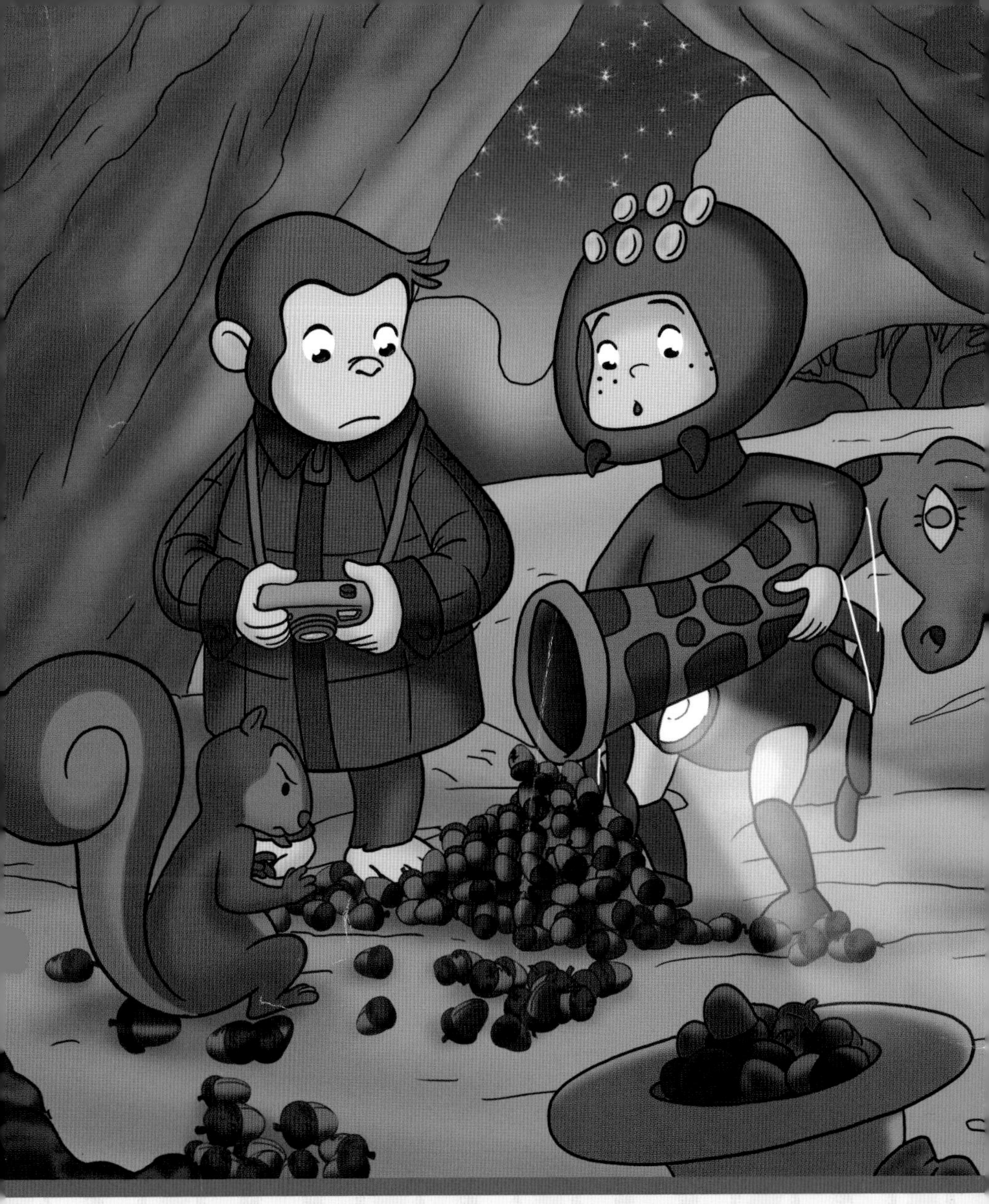

There was no headless scarecrow!
It had been Jumpy all along.
Jumpy and his squirrel friends had taken
the hats to collect acorns.

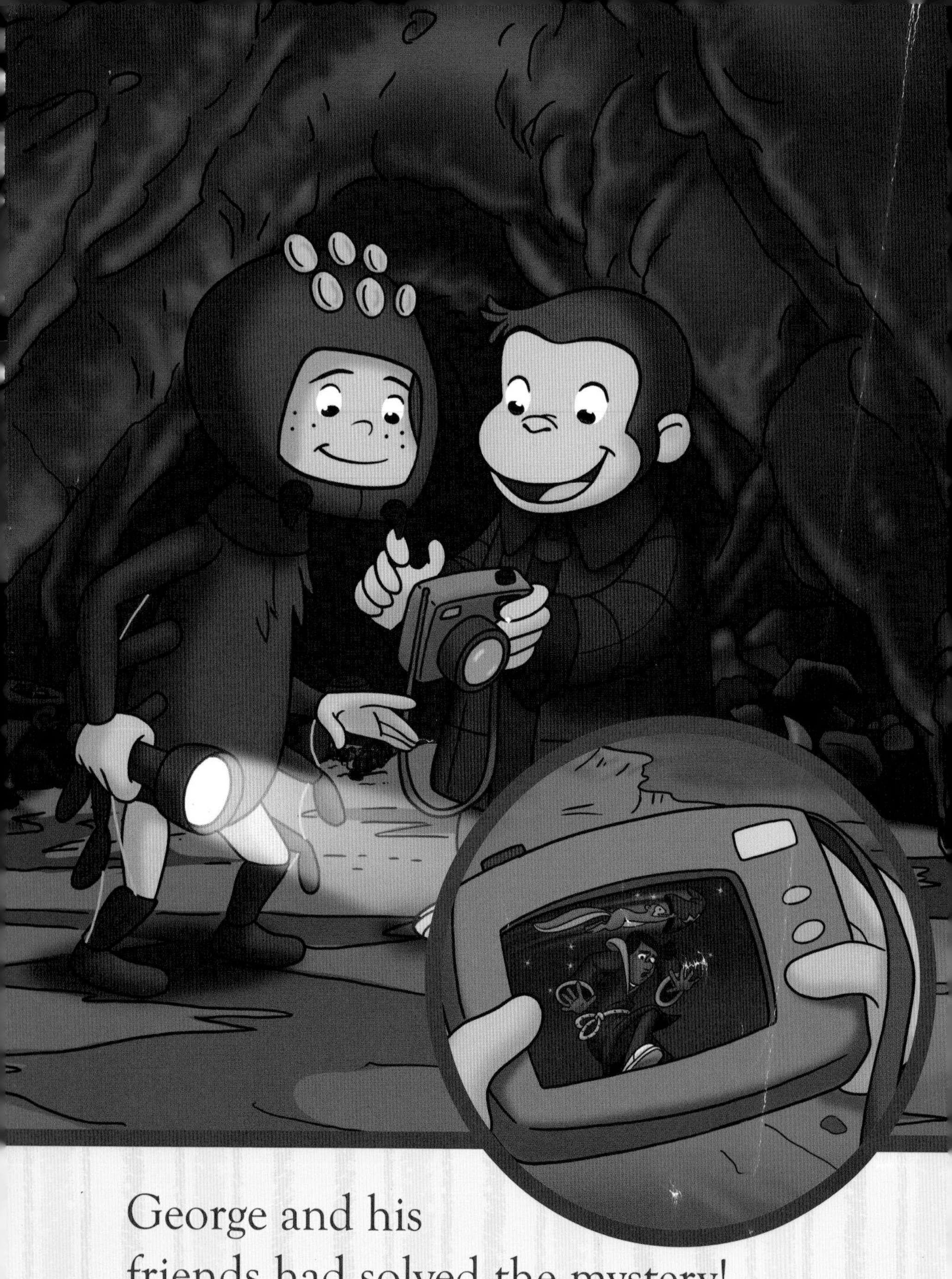

George and his
friends had solved the mystery!
And they even had proof to show
everyone the truth behind the Legend
of No Noggin.

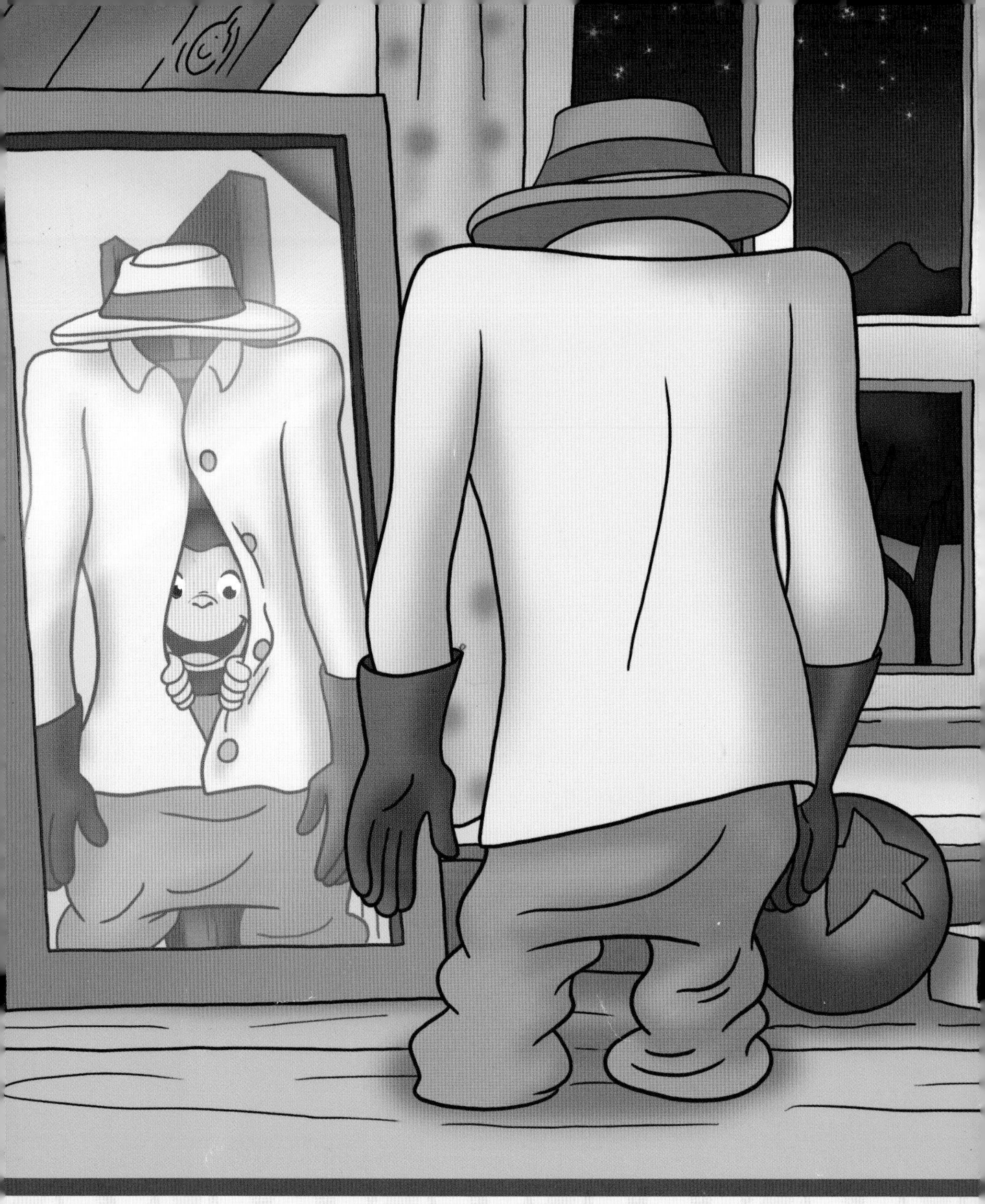

Well . . . maybe after Halloween. Now it was time for George to put on his costume and join his friends for trick-or-treating.

Make Your Own Pumpkin Head

One of the best parts of Halloween is putting on a new costume. With these instructions, you can make a pumpkin mask that will fool anyone. Just be sure No Noggin isn't around to steal it!

What you need:
- a sheet of paper
- a paper plate
- scissors
- two pieces of string
- a hole punch
- a pencil
- markers, paints, or crayons
- tape or glue

Instructions:
1. On the piece of paper, use a pencil to trace your hand. Cut out your tracing and color it green. This will be your pumpkin stem!
2. Next, draw a face on the paper plate. It can be scary or silly, and it can have three eyes, a big mouth, or no nose! It's completely up to you!
3. Color your paper plate orange to look like a pumpkin.
4. Ask an adult to help you cut out two eyeholes and a mouth.
5. Tape or glue your stem to the top of the mask.
6. Punch one hole on each side of the mask, where the ears might be. Make sure there's enough room between the hole and the edge of the mask!
7. Tie a piece of string to each hole.

Now your mask is ready to wear! Ask someone to help you tie it on your head, and get ready to fool everyone with your very own pumpkin head.

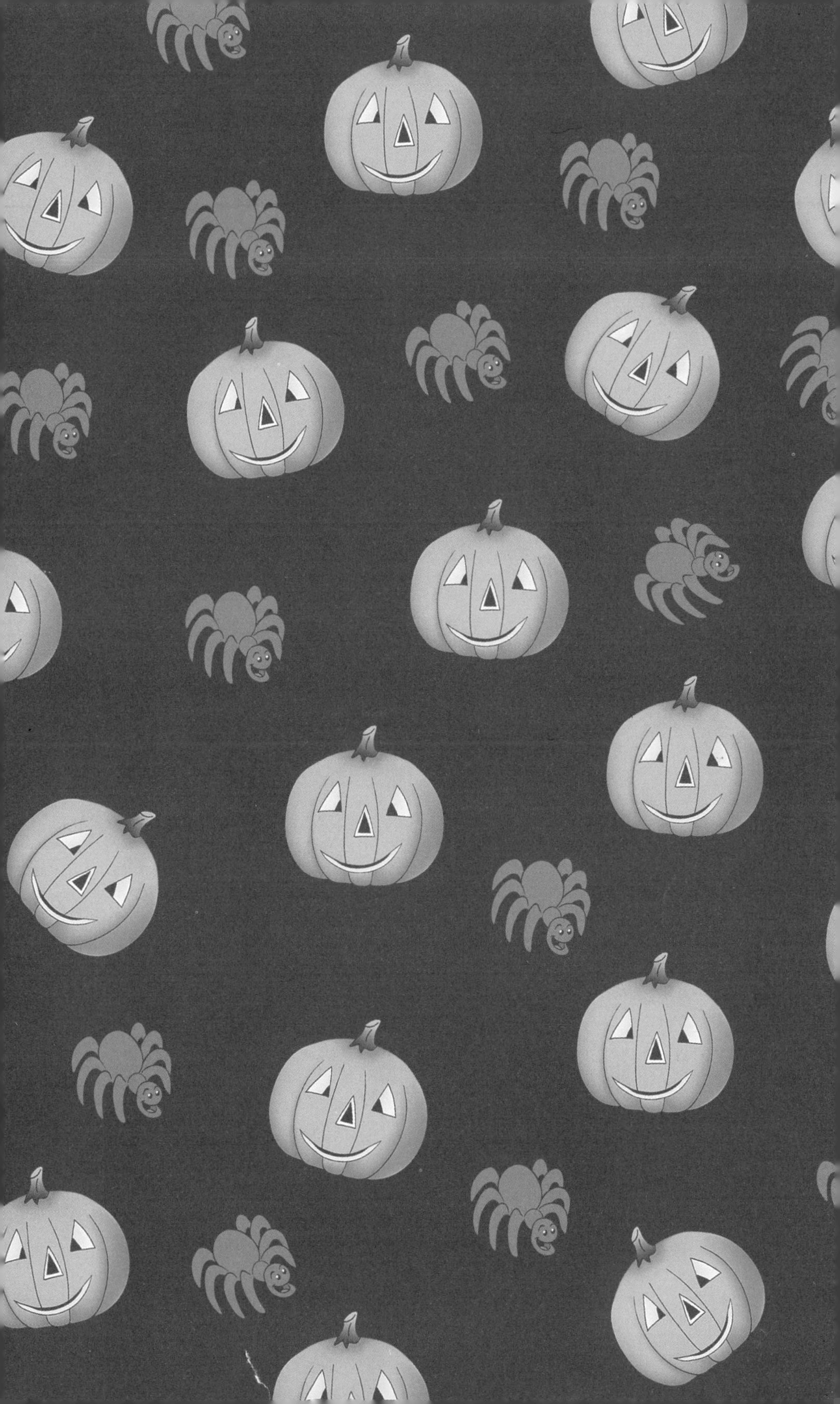

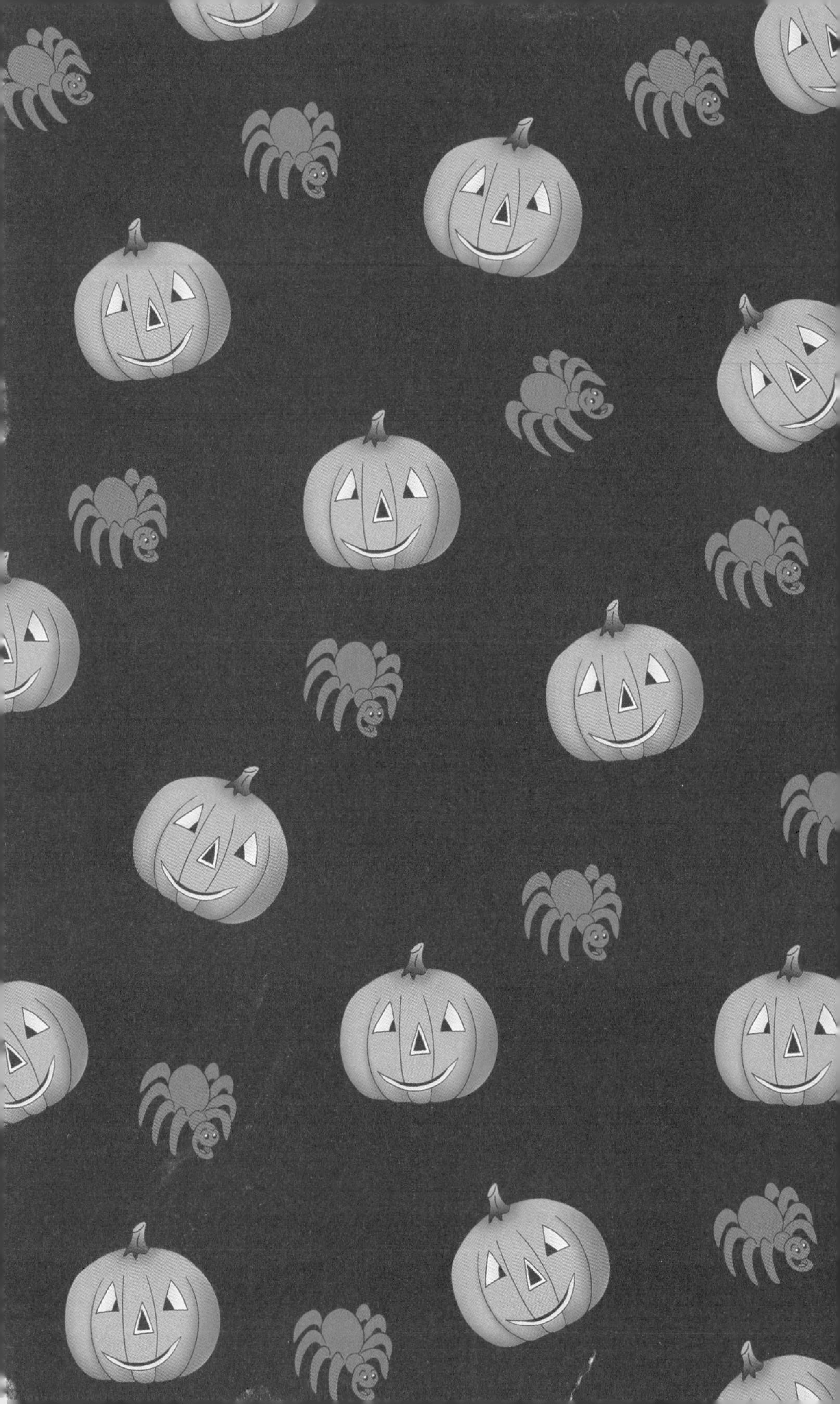